Emily's Runaway Imagination

Wham. Bang. Crash. This was too strange. A dog's howl, thunder, rain—these were easily explained, but this. . . . Emily jumped out of bed and looked out of the window. Through the lashing branches of the horse chestnut tree she could see a ghostly white figure moving across the barnyard. She shut her eyes and opened them again. The ghostly figure really was there. She could see it with her own eyes.

"June!" Emily cried. "Look!"

June leaned on the sill beside her. This time she had no matter-of-fact explanation. "Oh!" She clutched Emily's arm. "It's a ghost and it's coming closer!"

Enjoy all of
Beverly Cleary's books

Beverly Cleary

Emily's Runaway Imagination

ILLUSTRATED BY
Tracy Dockray

HarperTrophy®
An Imprint of HarperCollinsPublishers

Harper Trophy® is a registered trademark of
HarperCollins Publishers.

Emily's Runaway Imagination
Copyright © 1961 by Beverly Cleary
All rights reserved. Printed in the United States of
America. No part of this book may be used or reproduced
in any manner whatsoever without written permission
except in the case of brief quotations embodied in critical
articles and reviews. For information address
HarperCollins Children's Books,
a division of HarperCollins Publishers,
195 Broadway, New York, N.Y. 10007
Library of Congress Catalog Card Number: 61-10939
ISBN 978-0-380-70923-6
Typography by Amy Ryan
❖
Reillustrated Harper Trophy edition, 2008
Visit us on the World Wide Web!
www.harpercollinschildrens.com
19 20 BRR 30

CONTENTS

Emily's
Runaway
Imagination

1
Emily Goes To The Post Office

The things that happened to Emily Bartlett that year!

It seemed to Emily that it all began one bright spring day, a day meant for adventure. The weather was so warm Mama had let her take off her long stockings and put on her half socks for the first time since last fall. Breezes on her knees after a winter of stockings always made Emily feel as frisky as a spring lamb. The field that Emily could see from the kitchen window had turned blue with wild forget-me-nots and down in the pasture the trees, black silhouettes trimmed with abandoned bird nests throughout the soggy winter, were suddenly turning green.

Everywhere sap was rising, and Emily felt as if it was rising in her, too. This made it difficult for her to sit still long enough to write to her cousin Muriel, who lived in Portland and had so many wonderful things—things like fleece-lined bedroom slippers with kittens on the toes, cement sidewalks to roller-skate on, and a public library full of books.

"Finish your letter, Emily," said Mama, who was scrubbing out milk pans at the kitchen sink while the washing machine churned away on the back porch. "Then you can take it to the post office."

Emily looked up from her letter. "Mama,

I just know something wonderful is going to happen today," she said. "I can feel it in my bones."

Mama laughed. "Adventure is pretty scarce here in Pitchfork. I think your imagination is running away with you."

Mama often said this and whenever she did, Emily could just see herself hanging on for dear life in a buggy pulled pell-mell down Main Street by a frightened horse, the way a horse once ran away with Mama when she first came out West to teach school. All Mama's hairpins came out, her long black hair came tumbling down around her shoulders, and by the time someone stopped the horse she was a sight. Emily was always sorry she could not have been there to see the horse run away with Mama the way her imagination was supposed to run away with her.

Emily read Muriel's letter once more.

Dear Emily,
This week I went to the library. I got
Black Beauty. *It is about a horse. It is*
the best book I ever read. I read it three
times. I have to go now. Write soon.
Yours truly,
Muriel.
P.S. Mama sends her love.

It was not an easy letter to answer. Muriel was always writing about the library books she read—books like *Heidi* and *Toby Tyler*, which Emily had never even seen. Aunt Irene, Muriel's mother, said Muriel was a regular little bookworm.

Emily did not envy Muriel the fleece-lined bedroom slippers or the cement side-walk for roller-skating, but she did envy her that library. She longed to be a book-worm, although she did not think she would care to be called one. Unfortunately, the town of Pitchfork, Oregon, did not have a library. Oh, there were things to read—the Burgess *Bedtime Story* in the newspaper, Elson *Reader Book IV*, and the Sunday-school paper, but none of these qualified Emily to be a bookworm. Emily was not lucky like Muriel, who could ride a streetcar downtown to a big library full of hundreds, even thousands, of books, although of course Emily was lucky in other ways.

Emily was lucky because of Mama, who right now was sitting down to rest her feet while the washing machine did its work out on the back porch. Mama was so little she always wore high heels, even though she had a great big house to take care of. Tap-tap-tap went her heels all day long. Once, three years ago, during the war, when Mama had been an Honor Guard girl and had marched in a parade to get people to buy Liberty Bonds, she had lost one of her heels right in the middle of the parade, but that did not stop Mama. She had marched tap-bump, tap-bump all the way down Main Street to help sell Liberty Bonds. Mama had spunk.

It was funny about Mama's being so small, because Daddy was big and strong and handsome. Once when he was just out of high school, some men came out from Portland and told Daddy he should be a prize-fighter, but Daddy said, no, thank you, he would rather be a farmer. This was lucky, because sometimes when Emily got into an argument with one of the girls at school, she settled it by saying, "My father could have been a prize-fighter if he'd wanted to, but he didn't want to. So there!"

Emily was lucky in her ancestors, too. They had been pioneers, and whenever things were hard, Mama always said, "Remember your pioneer ancestors." Emily had always liked the stories of their trip across the plains in their covered wagons. Now Emily's pioneer ancestors were all dead and buried in the weedy little cemetery called Mountain Rest, but she did have Grandpa and Grandma Slater, Mama's parents, right here in Pitchfork.

Emily was lucky in many ways. She was lucky in the house she lived in, a house with three balconies, a cupola, banisters just right for sliding down, and the second bathtub in Yamhill County. Emily did not know who owned the first bathtub, but having the second bathtub was still pretty important. It showed that their house, known as the old Bartlett place, was very old.

The house had thirteen rooms, half of them empty of furniture, and people often asked, "Don't the three of you rattle around all by yourselves in that great big house?" Emily did not think she and Mama and Daddy rattled around at all. They moved around, it was true, but they did not rattle.

Sometimes they slept in the downstairs bedrooms, sometimes in one or another of the upstairs bedrooms, and often on summer nights they slept out on one of the balconies under the stars. Sometimes they set up their Christmas tree in the sitting room and sometimes in the parlor. Mama said not many people could be gypsies in their own house.

"Mama, I wish Pitchfork had a library," said Emily. "It isn't fair for Muriel to have all the books."

"That's the way it goes," said Mama, rubbing her foot. "This world's goods are never evenly divided."

"But just suppose we did have a library. Then I could read *Black Beauty* and fairy stories—anything I wanted. Suppose Pitchfork had a library with one hundred thousand books!"

"There goes your imagination again," said Mama.

"But it does seem as if library books could

be evened up a little." Emily, who was often lonely, spoke wistfully. The Bartlett front porch was just inside the town limits, but the rest of the house, and the barn and fields, were in the country, and there was no one near for Emily to play with.

"Emily, you are right," said Mama suddenly. "Go get the tablet of linen paper. I am going to write a letter for you to mail."

"Who to?" asked Emily.

"The state library in Salem," said Mama, who believed in never putting off until tomorrow what she could do today. "Times are changing. Other towns are getting libraries—there is already one in Cornelius. There's no reason why Pitchfork can't keep up with the times. Just think, Emily, there are people who have lived here all their lives who have never seen a library. And now I'm going to find out how to get a library started."

"Mama!" cried Emily joyfully and, forgetting her own letter, she ran for the tablet of good writing paper. Let the washing machine churn on the back porch! Oh *dear*, oh *dear*, oh *dear*, it seemed to complain as it labored. Pooh to the washing machine! Let it complain. Mama was writing a letter, an important letter, and Emily was going to get to mail it.

Soon Mama had the letter written and addressed in her neat schoolteacher handwriting. Emily licked a stamp, placed it on the envelope, and pounded it down with her fist so it would be sure to stick tight. This was a very important postage stamp and it must not fall off on its way to Salem, the capital of Oregon.

Emily put on her coat and went skipping off to the post office. Her knees, exposed for the first time in months, felt chilly, but she did not care. She was off to adventure. She would mail the letter and spread the glad tidings that maybe there was going to be a library in town. A library that might even have *Black Beauty*.

Emily heard a bark and found Prince, the collie, loping after her. "Come on, Prince," she called, glad to have the company of the good-natured dog.

Prince was the Bartletts' loafing dog. It was old Bob, a bobtailed black shepherd, who worked around the place, rounding up the cows and keeping an eye on things. Daddy always said old Bob was as smart as most people. Not Prince. He had just turned up one day, and although Daddy had published a notice in the weekly paper, the *Pitchfork Report*, no one claimed him. Daddy said he could see why, but he also said another dog around the place didn't make much differ-ence one way or another, and even though the collie wasn't good for much, he did seem to be a prince of a fellow. The dog stayed and was named Prince. Now as Emily pat-ted his head, he wagged his plumy tail, as if he too felt the arrival of spring and was eager for adventure.

Together they traveled over the board sidewalk, past Pete Ginty's carpenter shop and Fong Quock's house and vegetable garden, until they turned the corner by the Masonic Hall. Then they were on Main Street, which was paved and had a cement sidewalk.

Emily was not the only one in Pitchfork who felt as if the sap was rising within. Bertie Young, the barber's son, came running down the sidewalk, rolling an old automobile tire in front of him. When he reached Emily he stopped. "Hello, Emily," he said, bending over. "Want to smell my haircut?"

Emily inhaled deeply. *M-m-m.* Lilac! Bertie had the fanciest-smelling haircuts of anyone in town.

After Bertie had gone on, Emily met her

cousin June Bartlett, who was going to the drugstore for her mother. June's barrette was sliding out of her hair, but she did not care. That was the difference between Emily and June. Emily cared about things. June did not. This was sometimes discouraging to Emily, but in Pitchfork cousins were expected to like one another and no nonsense about it.

"Guess what!" said Emily. "Maybe we are going to have a library right here in Pitchfork. I'm going to mail a letter about it right now."

"You mean with books?" asked June.

"Of course," answered Emily, exasperated. What else could be in a library?

"We have a Tarzan book at home," said June, and went on her way to the drugstore, stepping on all the cracks as she went.

When Emily and Prince reached the post office, Emily took one last look at the important letter addressed to the state librarian before she poked it through the slot. Because the window was not yet open, she leaned over and peeked through the slot at her Uncle Avery, who was not only post-master but mayor of Pitchfork as well. He was busy cranking letters through the machine that postmarked the envelopes.

"Uncle Avery," she said through the slot. "Guess what! Maybe Pitchfork is going to have a library."

"Well now, won't that be nice," answered Uncle Avery, cranking away at the postmark-ing machine.

As Emily was about to leave the post office, she ran into Fong Quock, the only Chinese left of the many who had once lived around Pitchfork. Emily felt shy when she was with the old man, even though he was her closest neighbor and she was really very fond of him. She had known him all her life, and Daddy had known him almost all his life, too. Fong Quock had come from China when he was a young man and Daddy was a boy. He had settled near the Bartlett house, where he took in washing and raised vegetables to sell. When one of the Bartlett boys had a stomachache from eating too many green apples, or broke his arm falling out of the haymow, Grandma Bartlett had always sent Fong Quock for the doctor, and off he would go, lickety-split, with his queue flying and his slippers flapping. Now of course he no longer wore a queue or slippers. He did not take in washing, either. He had recently sold the confectionery store where the people of Pitchfork had for many years bought their all-day suckers and ice-cream sodas. He dressed like everyone else and was too old to go lickety-split. Daddy and all Emily's aunts and uncles loved Fong Quock, and no wonder. He was such a kind, jolly little man.

Emily was ashamed to feel shy with Fong Quock, but the truth of the matter was she had a hard time understanding him. His English was not very good, and no matter how hard he tried he never could pronounce the letter *r*. It always sounded like *l*. Mama said she could certainly sympathize. When she studied German in high school back East she never could learn to pronounce *r* in the proper German way.

"Hello, Missy," said Fong Quock, who called all the little girls in Pitchfork Missy.

"Good morning, Mr. Quock," answered Emily politely.

Prince, who always liked attention, went over to the old man and wagged his tail hopefully. Fong Quock patted his head and said, "Nice doggie. You name Plince, eh, fellow?"

Without thinking, Emily said politely—at

least she meant to speak politely, "No, it's Prince, Mr. Quock." And the words were no sooner out of her mouth than she realized what a dreadful mistake she had made. Fong Quock had been trying to say Prince, but he could not pronounce the *r*. She felt her cheeks grow hot. She would not have hurt the old man's feelings for anything in the world.

"Yes," said Fong Quock, nodding as his wrinkled face crinkled with amusement. "Plince."

Everyone in the post office laughed and so did Fong Quock. He threw back his head and laughed as if he thought the whole thing a huge joke. But Emily did not think it was funny, not one bit. She was so embarrassed and humiliated that she turned and fled.

Prince came padding after her. "What did you have to come tagging along for?" she asked, forgetting that she had been eager to share her feeling of adventure. From inside the post office she could hear people laughing—laughing at her.

Emily was not anxious to meet anyone

who had been in the post office, so she decided to pay a visit to Grandpa and Grandma Slater in their store until the coast was clear.

On the false front of Grandpa's store were the words *W. A. Slater, General Merchandise.* How Emily loved Grandpa's store! One side, Grandpa's side, was full of groceries—shelves of canned goods, bins of bulk foods to be weighed out on scales, a wheel of Tillamook cheese under an isinglass cover, a red coffee grinder, and a little chopper for cutting off plugs of chewing tobacco. Emily liked Grandma's side, the dry-goods side, even better. It was filled with bolts of dress goods, spools of ribbon, a revolving case of sewing thread, skeins of embroidery cotton. The back of the store was least interesting—just overalls and work shoes and a big drum of coal oil. One of the nicest things about the store was that, although the Bartletts paid for everything they took, Emily was the only girl in town who was allowed to go behind the counters.

Grandpa was leaning over the counter figuring something on the back of an envelope, probably something called profit and loss. When Grandpa introduced Emily to someone he always said, "This is Emily. She's the only granddaughter I've got, but she's a humdinger."

"Well hello, Emily," he said, looking up from his envelope. "I'll pay you a nickel if you can sit still for five minutes."

Emily smiled. This was an offer Grandpa made almost every time she came to the store and usually she sat on a chair for five minutes by the clock to earn the nickel. She was saving up her sitting-still nickels to buy Mama a rotary eggbeater, the kind that would beat eggs and whip cream when you turned

the handle around and around. This morning, however, she decided against earning a nickel and in favor of going upstairs to the rooms where Grandpa and Grandma lived. She would say hello to Grandma and avoid anyone who might be coming to the store from the post office.

Upstairs was the best part of all—Grandma's millinery room, where Grandma trimmed hats for the ladies of Pitchfork—and it was there that Emily found her grandmother, her mouth full of pins, trimming a white leghorn hat with beautiful pink ribbon bows. Grandma nodded and smiled through her mouthful of pins. Dear gentle Grandma, who always smelled of violets.

Emily heard the merry ring of the cash register downstairs as Grandpa waited on his customers. To pass the time until they left she amused herself exploring the millinery room—the deep round boxes of untrimmed hats, bolts of veiling, boxes of flowers. There were velvet violets for winter hats, garlands of daisies and poppies, bunches of hard red cherries that rattled when Emily picked them up, stiff little nosegays of forget-me-nots, even artificial wheat, although why anybody would want to trim a hat with anything so ordinary as wheat Emily could not understand. And the ostrich plumes! Each beautiful curling plume lay in its own question-mark-shaped compartment in a big box. Grandma had dozens of lovely plumes, which she said would surely come back in style. Grandma said if you kept a thing seven years, it was bound to come back in style.

At last Grandma took the pins out of her mouth. "How are you today, Emily," she asked.

"Just fine, Grandma." Emily stabbed a pincushion with a hatpin. "Grandma, do you know maybe Pitchfork is going to have a library? Mama wrote a letter to the state library this morning and I mailed it."

"Well now, wouldn't that be nice?" Grandma deftly twisted a length of ribbon into a crisp bow. "Other towns have libraries, I've heard. There's no reason why Pitchfork can't keep up with the times."

"That is just what Mama said," Emily told her grandmother. And then deciding that the coast must be clear by now, because the store was quiet, she added, "Good-bye, Grandma."

Grandma smiled. "You didn't pay me a very long visit today."

Emily did not want to tell Grandma that she was hiding from the people who had been in the post office. She said, "I'll be back soon." Then she ran downstairs, where Grandpa was weighing out tea for a customer. "Good-bye, Grandpa," she said.

Grandpa paused with his hand above the scales and looked at Emily with what she always thought of as his twinkly look. "Good-bye, Emily," he said. "You and Plince come again soon."

Emily felt herself blush once more. "Now Grandpa, you stop it," she said, and hurried out of the store with Prince trotting after her. So someone had already told Grandpa about her mistake! Well, she might have known.

Emily soon discovered that Grandpa was not the only person who had been told. Everyone Emily met on the street said, "Good morning, Emily. Hello there, Plince"—George A. Barbee, who had the longest gray beard in Pitchfork; Mrs. Warty Thompson, who played the piano at the picture show on Saturday night; the man who ran the feed store—everybody. Emily was so embarrassed that she hurried on without even stopping to spread the glad tidings about the important letter she had just mailed.

She decided to go home the long way around, because she could not face passing Fong Quock's house. She did not want to run into him again for a long, long time, not until everyone in Pitchfork had stopped laughing at her thoughtless mistake. She went down a side street past the garage and the warehouse full of farm machinery for sale, and turned onto Locust Street at the corner by the blacksmith shop.

Emily always took pains to speak nicely to the blacksmith since that Friday afternoon at school when her class, which always studied the poets during the last hour of the school week, read *The Village Blacksmith* by Henry Wadsworth Longfellow, a poet with a long gray beard like George A. Barbee's. In the poem were the lines:

And the muscles of his brawny arms
Are strong as iron bands.

After that day any boy who passed the blacksmith shop always yelled:

"And the muscles of his scrawny arms
Are strong as rubber bands."

This made Emily feel so sorry for Mr. Wilcox, the blacksmith, that she always spoke to him nicely, in what she hoped was an admiring voice. Mr. Wilcox always seemed glad to see her and once he made her a ring out of a horseshoe nail. This morning she found him working on a plowshare. "Good morning, Mr. Wilcox," she said through the open door.

"Hello there, Emily," answered Mr. Wilcox. "I see you have your dog Plince with you this fine morning."

Even Mr. Wilcox, her good friend Mr. Wilcox, was teasing her. Emily did not know what to say so she said, "Yes . . . uh, well, I guess I better be going," and hurried down the road with Prince padding after her.

When she reached the farm she found her mother hanging out the washing on the lines strung between the tank house and the woodshed. Mama pinched a clothespin over a dish towel on the line. "Well, Emily, did you and Plince have a nice walk?"

"Mama!" cried Emily. "How did *you* know?"

Mama laughed. "Mrs. Warty Thompson telephoned me about the next meeting of the Ladies' Civic Club. She told me she ran into Fong Quock on Main Street and he told her. He thought it was a huge joke."

"I suppose everybody on the line was listening in," said Emily crossly, because she did not like being laughed at. The Bartletts were on a five-party telephone line, and Mama was always careful never to say on the telephone anything that she was not willing for the whole town to hear.

"I did hear the sound of some receivers being lifted while I was talking," said Mama with a smile.

Emily heaved an exasperated sigh. "Now everybody in the whole world will have to know."

Mama shook out a pillowcase and pinned it to the clothesline. "You know how it is in a small town," she said. "People talk."

They certainly did, thought Emily. They talked on Main Street, they talked in Grandpa's store, they talked on the party line. The trouble was, they did not talk about the right things. She wanted everybody to spread the glad tidings about the library and what did they talk about? Plince. She might as well start calling the dog Plince, because from now on everyone else would.

And how was she ever going to get to be a bookworm and read *Black Beauty* like Muriel if people wouldn't talk about the library?

2

Mama's Elegant Party

Mama was so busy and so excited this morning that she burned the toast. Emily was so excited that she did not want to eat toast, especially toast that had been scraped.

"Now Emily," said Mama, "it is wicked to waste food. Just think of the starving Armenians."

Emily would have been delighted to give her toast to one of the starving Armenians she had been hearing so much about lately, but since there were no starving Armenians in Pitchfork, she nibbled away at her toast. Scraped toast on the day Mama was having a party, an elegant party! The members of the Ladies' Civic Club were coming for luncheon—*luncheon* on a farm where the Bartletts always had dinner at noon.

Mama was going to steer the conversation around to the subject of a library for Pitchfork. The state library really had answered her letter and had offered to send seventy-five books at a time, but first the town must find a place to keep the books and someone to act as librarian. Mama had more ideas. If all the people of Pitchfork donated what books they owned, there might be enough books to start a permanent library.

Of course Emily was eager for the party to begin. The Bartletts, who always rose early, because Daddy had to milk the cows at five o'clock in the morning, had been busy. Emily wanted to do everything she could to make Mama's party a success. She had gone down to the pasture to gather buttercups and Johnny-jump-ups for the table. She had dug the maraschino cherries out of their tight little jar to put in the fruit salad. She had even gone to the drugstore for the ice cream the short way, at the risk of running into Fong Quock, because she wanted to hurry back to help Mama.

Daddy had killed some hens the day before and Mama had made chicken à la king with pimiento out of a can from Grandpa's store. She had made patty shells just like the ones she used to have back East. The trouble she had with those patty shells! The first batch refused to puff up and Emily had to take them out to feed to the chickens, because even though they had plenty of butter and flour on the farm, they could not waste food, because of the starving Armenians. Mama's angel food cake made up for the trouble with the patty shells. Even without a rotary beater to beat the egg whites it was as light as a feather. Mama said goodness only knew what she was going to do with all the left-over egg yolks.

"Pretty fancy food you're fixing," teased Daddy. "It seems like a lot of trouble for a bunch of women to get together just to gabble."

Mama was too busy to be teased. "I do hope this luncheon will be a success," was all she said, and whizzed around with the carpet sweeper and a dust cloth, while Daddy got out the scythe to cut the grass in front of the house. Emily followed and raked up the grass.

When Daddy worked his way over to the fence that separated the yard from the orchard, he swung the scythe through the grass and *whack* right into an overturned apple box that was hidden by the grass.

"That Goliath!" exclaimed Daddy. "I forgot about the apples he knocked over."

Then Emily remembered. Last winter Daddy had picked two boxes of apples. When he had pastured Goliath the bull in the orchard, he had set the boxes of apples over the fence to get them out of the bull's way. This had not stopped Goliath, who had managed to get his head over the wire fence and knock over the boxes. He took bites out of all the apples that did not roll out of his reach, and since the Bartletts had plenty of apples, and no one wanted to eat apples that had been nuzzled by a bull, the rest of the apples had lain rotting in the tall grass along with the windfalls that had dropped from the trees.

"Say, Emily," said Daddy, as he swung the scythe, "see if you can get rid of those apples so I can cut the rest of the grass."

"What shall I do with them?" asked Emily.

"Anything," answered Daddy. "Just get rid of them."

Emily examined the apples scattered in the grass. They were rotten now—brown and squashy rotten. She picked up an apple which had a rich cidery smell and tossed it over the fence into the orchard, where it landed with a plop and smelled even more cidery. Emily did not think Mama would like a lot of smelly rotten apples plopped over the fence when she was having an elegant party, so she decided that the thing to do was feed them to the hogs, who would probably enjoy them. Emily loved to pick an apple and bruise it by dragging it along a picket fence before she ate it. The juicy bruises were the best part of the apple. If a bruise tasted good to her, a whole rotten apple must taste delicious to a hog. Besides, Mama said it was wicked to waste food— think of the starving Armenians.

Emily found an old dishpan, which she filled with the squashy apples and lugged around to the back of the house and across the barnyard to the hogpen. There she found she could not climb up on the fence with the dishpan in her hands, so she opened the gate to dump the apples on the ground for the hogs.

The hogs were delighted. They squealed and rooted and snuffled at the apples and gobbled them up while Emily carefully closed the gate and ran back for more. As Emily dumped the second dishpanful of apples into the hogpen, she heard Mama calling from the back porch.

"Emily! Come on, it's time to get dressed!"

Was it that late already? Emily ran back to

the house as fast as she could go. She washed hastily at the kitchen sink and ran upstairs to put on her best dress and her Mary Janes, which she discovered were almost too small for her. When she came downstairs some of the ladies were already coming up the boardwalk between the two privet hedges that led to the house.

How beautiful Mama looked in her gray silk with the white ruffle at the neck, as she swished down the hall to answer the door. And how lovely all the ladies looked in their dress-up dresses and spring hats— some of Grandma's nicest hats. There was Mrs. Archer, the banker's wife in a black straw with orange poppies. A whole dozen silk poppies had gone into the trimming of that hat. And Mrs. Twitchell, the mother of Arlene Twitchell, the prettiest girl in town, in a hat Grandma had already retrimmed twice. Emily thought it was still a beautiful

hat, but the ladies of Pitchfork said it was a shame the way Mrs. Twitchell wore the same hat year after year while Arlene had all those new clothes. Mrs. Warty Thompson wore a toque of flowered silk, and Mrs. George Thompson a hat everyone knew she had trimmed herself. Her husband's prune crop had not brought any price at all last year.

At last there were nineteen hats lying on Great-grandmother Bartlett's four-poster bed in the downstairs bedroom. Mama's company had examined the place cards around the big dining-room table, which had enough leaves added so that twenty places could be set. Mama had not extended the table as much as this since last summer, when she had cooked dinner for the crew of men who came to help Daddy bale the hay. How elegant everyone looked and how refined the hum of conversation sounded— quite different from the sweaty overalls and loud voices of the hay balers. Mama's party was going to be a success. Emily could tell.

Emily did not want to miss a thing, but

Mama was depending on her to help serve the chicken à la king and fruit salad. "Mama, do I serve the plates from the right or the left?" Emily whispered anxiously. "I always get mixed up."

Mama's face was flushed and she was trying not to spatter chicken à la king on her good gray silk. "From the right—no, I mean the left," was her flustered answer.

Emily carried the plates, two by two, into the dining room and served them with great care. It would be dreadful to dump creamed chicken in someone's lap. When the last plate was served and Mama herself was seated at the head of the table, Emily climbed up on the kitchen stool to eat her own meal off the drainboard. It had taken every chair the Bartletts owned and a few borrowed ones besides to seat the members of the club.

The conversation in the dining room hushed as the ladies began to eat Mama's delicious cooking. There were polite little murmurs of, "The best I've ever tasted!" and, "You must let me have your recipe," when Emily became aware, as did the guests, of noises outside. And what a racket it was—squeals and grunts and the barking of dogs. Emily had never heard anything like it before.

"My land!" cried Mama. "What on earth is going on out there?"

Emily ran to the kitchen window, but she couldn't see a thing, because the woodshed was in the way. The squeals and grunts grew louder and the dogs barked furiously. And then a terrible thought occurred to Emily. Had she fastened the gate when she dumped the apples into the hogpen? Had she done what she had been told she must never, never do and left the gate open? She was sure she had closed it, but now she was not so sure she had fastened it. No matter how hard she tried, she could not remember. Mama had called, Emily had been in a hurry to get cleaned up before company came . . . she had a terrible feeling . . . oh, dear . . . if she had left the gate unfastened, Daddy was going to be pretty angry. Emily only hoped that if she had left the gate unfastened so the hogs got out, Daddy would wait until the ladies had gone home before he gave her a talking-to. Or he might even spank her!

All the guests had stopped talking to listen. Mama jumped up from the table and ran out on the back porch. Emily and the nineteen ladies followed. Mama ran down the back steps and along the walk to the barnyard, with Emily and the nineteen ladies right after her. This was terrible—all the ladies leaving Mama's luncheon instead of talking about the library.

And what a sight met their eyes! All

twelve hogs were running around the orchard squealing and snorting and grunting. Plince, as the whole town now called the collie, was standing on the steps of the tank house barking hysterically, while old Bob, who knew there was work to be done, ran after the hogs, barking and snapping at their heels to persuade them to go back to their pen.

Oh, thought Emily, how dreadful! She *had* left the gate unfastened. She saw Daddy standing in the barn door, staring at the hogs.

But wait! Something was wrong, terribly wrong with the hogs that old Bob had managed to herd into the barnyard. They were not really running. They were lurching and swaying and staggering. Poor old Bob was working as hard as he could to round them up, but they no longer paid any attention to him.

"What on earth—" began Mama and seemed to have no words left.

The ladies recovered sufficiently from their surprise to begin to talk. "Did you ever . . ." "What under the sun . . ." "Never in my born days . . ." Then someone tittered and the rest of the ladies laughed, too. The hogs did look funny.

Emily also thought they looked funny, but she could not laugh, because she was so worried. What on earth had she done to Daddy's hogs? And in a year when he hoped to get a good price for them, too! And then before her very eyes one of the hogs keeled over and lay still.

Emily watched her father run down the ramp from the barn and try to chase a hog back into the pen. It paid no attention, but went lurching across the barnyard until it bumped into the watering trough. Then it fell over and lay still, even though old Bob

stood barking at it. There goes another one, thought Emily miserably.

"If I didn't know better," said Mrs. Archer, "I would say those hogs are tipsy."

"What a ridiculous idea," said Mrs. Twitchell. None of the ladies of Pitchfork approved of strong drink.

One hog, the one named Brutus, the biggest of them all, came staggering toward Mama's company. The ladies shrieked and retreated behind the picket fence while the hog stood swaying uncertainly and looking at them with its little beady eyes. It gave one tired grunt and one by one its legs seemed to fold up until it collapsed in a heap. Another one was gone.

"Well, I never!" exclaimed the wife of the druggist.

Another hog, the Hampshire sow Daddy had bought because it won first prize at the Livestock Exposition in Portland, tried to climb the steps of the tank house, fell, got up, and wandered off in an uncertain way that sent the ladies into a gale of giggles. Old Bob snapped at its heels, but the hog did not seem to notice. It was a happy-looking hog and it kept on going, which was encouraging to Emily.

"I don't care," said Mrs. Archer most disapprovingly. "Those hogs *are* tipsy. I'm positive."

Emily thought this was a terrible thing to say about Daddy's nice fat hogs. She was worried, too, because if Mrs. Archer disapproved of Daddy's hogs she might keep right on disapproving of other things, including Mama's plans for a library.

"Why, Sybil, how could any hogs of ours get tipsy?" Mama sounded hurt that Mrs. Archer could think such a thing.

"I don't know, Lydia," said Mrs. Archer, "but I do know they are tipsy."

"You know, Sybil," said Mrs. Twitchell, "I believe you're right. They *are* tipsy."

"Tipsy!" exclaimed Mrs. George Thompson. "They are just plain drunk."

"Of course I am right," said Mrs. Archer. "All those hogs need is to sober up."

"But that is ridiculous," protested Mama, anxious to defend the Bartlett honor. "How could our hogs get drunk?"

"I—I think I must have forgotten to latch the gate when I fed them some rotten apples this morning," ventured Emily, although she did not see what this could have to do with such strange behavior.

"You did!" exclaimed Mama. "Emily, did you really feed the hogs rotten apples?"

Still not understanding what she had done, Emily nodded miserably.

"Why, rotten apples would ferment," said Mama. "It was just like feeding the hogs hard cider. And then they got out into the orchard and ate more rotten apples that were lying on the ground—"

"I didn't mean to get them drunk," said Emily. "I thought they might like the apples for a change."

"They certainly did," said Mrs. Archer, "and made a beeline for more."

"Well, I'll be jiggered," said Mama, and suddenly she sat down on the back steps and went off into a gale of laughter. She sat there and laughed until she cried.

To Emily's amazement the rest of the ladies joined in. They tittered and giggled and laughed and wiped their eyes. They stopped laughing, held their sides, gasped for breath, and started all over again.

Emily was indignant. She did not think it was funny. It was terrible—all Daddy's beautiful Hampshire hogs drunk, and in a year when he hoped to get a high price for them.

"Mama, you said it was wicked to waste

food, because of the starving Armenians," said Emily reproachfully, "and so I didn't want to waste the apples, even if they were rotten."

"Oh, Emily," gasped Mama, and became helpless with laughter all over again. Emily knew what she was thinking. Emily's imagination had run away with her again.

Out in the barnyard the squeals and grunts subsided as one by one the hogs sagged to the ground, fast asleep.

"Dead drunk. Every last one of them," said Sybil Archer, and all the ladies went off into another gale of laughter.

"Oh, dear!" exclaimed Mama, when the ladies seemed to have no more laughter left in them. "Our food will all be cold."

"Never mind," said Mrs. Archer as the ladies went into the house. "I haven't had such a good laugh for years."

As Emily stood looking at the havoc she

had wrought she decided she was not hungry after all, not even for chicken in patty shells and fruit salad with maraschino cherries. Miserably she watched her father coming across the barnyard toward her. He stopped to nudge Brutus with his toe, but Brutus only flicked an ear, twitched his curly tail, and did not budge.

Emily remembered her pioneer ancestors and was brave. She sat down on the back steps to wait. From inside the house came another burst of laughter. Then came the sound of Mrs. Archer's voice. "I have never in all my born days seen anything so funny. . . ."

Daddy sat down beside Emily. "I meant to fasten the gate, but I guess I didn't," she said in a small voice.

"Well, Emily," said Daddy with a grin, "you know better than to leave a gate open."

How well Emily knew the rules! Never leave a gate open. Never walk uphill behind a load of hay. Never go into the field where the bull was pastured.

Inside, Mama's guests were busy talking over what they had just seen. There was no doubt about it. They were having a good time, a hilarious time, but they were not talking about a library.

"You know," Daddy went on, "I have an idea your feeding those rotten apples to the hogs is going to be the making of your mother's party. You've given her friends something to talk about and they aren't going to forget it."

Daddy was right. Mama always said people in a small town never forgot anything. Look at the way Prince's name had been changed to Plince.

"I guess we'll skip a spanking." Daddy leaned over and rubbed his chin against Emily's cheek. He had a good smell, a smell of freshly plowed earth. "You're getting pretty big to spank anyway," he said.

That was the nicest thing anyone had said to Emily for a long time. Too big to spank! A real milestone had been reached.

Inside, Mama's guests talked and laughed. It was easy to tell by the sounds that floated out that even though the chicken à la king was cold the party was a success, just as Mama had hoped it would be.

"Gabble, gabble, gabble," said Daddy with a chuckle. "You just wait. Your mother will have them all talking about a library before you know it."

"You don't think she's forgotten?" asked Emily.

"Not your mother," answered Daddy. "And do you want to know something? The Ladies' Civic Club is having such a good time it is going to agree to anything your mother suggests. You'll see."

And the wonderful part was, Daddy was

right. Emily was sure of it.

"And now how about fixing some of your mother's fancy cooking for your hungry dad?" suggested Daddy.

Emily discovered she was hungry after all. Besides, the kitchen was such a good place from which to eavesdrop on the dining room.

3
Emily's
Snow-White Steed

The Ladies' Civic Club had agreed with Mama that a library would be a good thing for Pitchfork. They were busy trying to find a place for the library when one day Emily received a letter from her cousin Muriel in Portland, a letter written on pink paper and mailed in a pink envelope. Muriel never wrote on tablet paper. She always wrote on stationery that came in a box.

Emily sat at the kitchen table reading the

letter while Mama thumbed through the new *Ladies' Home Journal* which Daddy had brought from the post office with the morning mail. The letter read:

> *Dear Emily,*
> *Mama says we are coming out to Pitchfork*
> *for Decoration Day. Saturday I went to*
> *the library. I got* Black Beauty *again. I*
> *wish we had a horse. You are lucky. On*
> *Decoration Day I would like to ride a*
> *horse on your farm.*
> *Yours truly,*
> *Muriel*

Well! This was news. Here Emily thought Muriel was lucky because she could go to the library and because her father owned an automobile, a Maxwell; but no, now it was Emily who was lucky because she had horses. That owning a horse was particularly fortunate had never occurred to Emily because everyone who owned a farm owned a horse or two, and many people who lived out in the country still came to town in buggies pulled by horses. Every day a horse-drawn hack from the livery stable drove to the depot to bring train passengers back to Main Street. Pitchfork was not, as some people said, a one-horse town.

Emily was much prouder of the Bartletts' tractor, which had its name, Big Mogul, painted on its sides, than she was of Pick and Lady, the horses. Sometimes she rode one of the horses around bareback, but she had never thought much about it one way or another. Riding Big Mogul with Daddy at the throttle was much more exciting, even more exciting than riding in an automobile, and Emily dearly loved to ride in an auto-mobile.

When Emily got to ride the merry-go-round at the State Fair, she never chose to ride on anything as ordinary as a horse. For her first ride she always chose a lion. Riding up and down and round and round on a lion while the calliope played was exciting. If she was lucky enough to have a second ride, she chose the rooster, because riding a rooster was funny. There was nothing exciting or funny about riding an ordinary everyday horse.

A fly buzzed over the oilcloth on the kitchen table. Mama dropped the *Journal* and picked up the flyswatter. "That pesky fly!" she said. Mama was death on flies. "There," she said, when she had disposed of the fly. "What does Muriel say?"

"They are coming here for Decoration Day," answered Emily, although this was hardly news. Both the city Bartletts and the country Bartletts, like other Pitchfork families, always got together on the thirtieth of May for a trip to the Mountain Rest

Cemetery. There they pulled weeds and raked leaves and left the graves of their pioneer ancestors tidy for another year. It was an occasion Emily always enjoyed, but now she wondered if she was going to get to enjoy it this year. "Muriel says she wants to ride a horse when she comes out here. She has been reading *Black Beauty* again."

"That's nice," said Mama absently, because she was studying the latest styles from back East. Then she looked up from her magazine. "I hope she won't be disappointed because we have plow horses instead of saddle horses."

Emily had not thought of this. She began to wonder what sort of horse Muriel, who had always been timid about going into the barn and who did not care for the smell of manure, would expect to ride. A beautiful black horse, obviously, from the title of the book she had read. Emily wished the library would hurry up and get started so the state library could send Pitchfork a copy of *Black Beauty* to help her know what she was up against. She was sure of one thing. Pick and Lady were not good enough for a city girl like Muriel, who knew about horses from reading books. Besides, they weren't black. They were white.

Just before supper when Emily went out to gather some eggs, she wandered into the barn where Daddy was milking with his head pressed against the cow's flank. "Nita, Juanita, ask thy soul if we should part," sang Daddy, who always said his cows gave milk better when he sang. *Ching-choo, ching-choo* went the sound of the milk in the pail, while several barn cats watched the stream of milk hungrily. When Daddy heard Emily, he stopped milking into the bucket and squirted milk at the cats, who opened their mouths and caught it. He knew this was a sight Emily enjoyed.

Emily climbed up on the partition between the stalls of Pick and Lady and looked down at them. The two horses were not even white, not really white. They might be called white, but in reality they were a dingy yellowish color and their tails were streaked with mud. And although the Bartletts had an old saddle hanging in the barn, Emily realized that neither horse could wear it, because their backs were too broad. It was all pretty discouraging.

As Decoration Day approached, Emily worried more and more about Pick and Lady not being good enough for a city girl who had read *Black Beauty*. Then one morning when Emily went out to feed the chickens she happened to notice Mama putting the towels to soak in the copper wash boiler on the back porch. Mama had filled the boiler with water, and now she was adding the Clorox.

"Does Clorox really make the towels whiter?" asked Emily.

"Yes, it does." Mama dumped in the towels and stirred them around with an old broom handle.

This was enough to inspire Emily. "Mama!"

she exclaimed. "Is it all right if I Clorox a horse?"

"Oh, Emily!" Mama laughed. "I don't know any reason why you shouldn't, but you'll have to ask your father."

Emily fed the chickens in a hurry that morning. She found her father in the machine shed tinkering with the harrow. "Daddy, is it all right if I Clorox a horse?" she asked.

Daddy did not laugh the way Mama had, but instead considered Emily's question seriously. "Yes, Emily," he said, "I expect you can as long as you rinse the horse good."

"Oh, thank you!" Emily was enormously relieved and ran off to school with a light heart. All her problems were taken care of. That day she had a terrible time remembering to find the lowest common denominator in arithmetic, because she was so busy thinking about the horse she was going to bleach. She would go to work on Lady and when she finished that horse was going to be as white as snow. It would be a beautiful snow-white steed with a long flowing mane and tail. As for a saddle—pooh! Who needed a saddle? Muriel could ride bareback like the beautiful lady Emily had once seen in a dog and pony show Grandpa had taken her to see in McMinnville. That would be much more romantic than riding with a saddle, even though Muriel would not be able to stand up on the horse the way the beautiful lady had. Muriel could mount Lady and fly like the wind across the barnyard with her long curls, the color of shavings in Pete Ginty's carpenter shop, streaming out behind her. Let's see, to bleach the horse she would need Clorox, a brush, water, a bucket, and lots of rags for drying the horse. And a currycomb. She would also need something to stand on—

Miss Plotkin, the teacher, rapped on her

desk with a ruler. "Emily Bartlett," she said sternly. "Stop woolgathering and pay attention to your arithmetic." Every time Miss Plotkin told Emily to stop woolgathering, Emily started picturing the birds gathering wool left on the barbed wire fences by the sheep and building lovely soft wool-lined nests for their babies, and there she was— woolgathering all over again. "Emily—" said Miss Plotkin with a warning note in her voice. Emily paid attention. She did not want to be sent to the cloakroom.

The minute Emily was released from school she ran home, where she found her mother making a batch of pie crust in the pantry. "Mama, Daddy said it is all right for me to Clorox a horse."

Mama looked concerned. "Change your clothes first. Put on your oldest dress. And be sure to read the directions on the label and dilute the Clorox. You mustn't use it straight from the bottle."

"Yes, Mama." Emily ran upstairs, changed to her oldest dress, slid down the banisters to save time, and gathered up her equipment, which she left in the barnyard by the watering trough. She took down a halter from a peg in the barn, ran down the hill, and skinned over the fence into the pasture. She had no trouble finding Lady, slipping the halter over her head, and leading her back to the watering trough.

Then Emily studied the label for directions on how to dilute the Clorox. Dish towels, sheets. No, that wasn't what she wanted. Scorch, mildew. No, Lady was neither scorched nor mildewed. There was not one word on the label about bleaching a horse. Emily reread the label and decided that the directions for stubborn stains came closest to filling her needs. She dipped a bucket of water out of the trough and carefully mixed the Clorox, making the mixture a little stronger than the directions called for, because Lady was such a big strong horse. Then she consulted the label once more. Soak fifteen minutes, it said. Now how on earth was she going to soak a horse fifteen minutes?

Emily stepped back to study Lady, who now seemed enormously large. Her tail and fetlocks—those fringes of hair around her feet—were the worst. The horse looked inquiringly at Emily with her large dark eyes. Emily decided she would need another bucket, so she found one in the barn and prepared a second mixture of bleach water. Then she tugged at Lady's hind foot until she lifted it and allowed Emily to guide it into the bucket.

"There!" she said. "You stand there with your foot in the bucket for fifteen minutes and your fetlock will be nice and white."

Lady answered with a whinny.

Then Emily sozzled the brush around in the other bucket, and standing on the edge of the watering trough, began to scrub Lady's back. The horse turned her head to look inquiringly at Emily. "Steady, girl," said Emily, hopping down to sozzle the brush again. Dirty water ran off the horse's back in little rivulets. Emily climbed back on the edge of the watering trough and rubbed and scrubbed. She jumped down and persuaded Lady to lift her hind foot out of the bucket. The fetlock really did come out white! She lugged the bucket around to the other hind foot which she grasped and lifted as hard as she could. It took Lady quite a while to decide she wanted to lift that foot and step into the bucket, but she finally gave in. Lady was a very patient horse.

Emily went on rubbing and scrubbing, rinsing and drying. She did not enjoy the smell of wet horse and Clorox, but she kept on working. The skin on her hands began to feel like crepe from being in the water so long. Then Lady stamped her foot and kicked over the bucket.

Emily, who was beginning to get tired, mixed another bucket of bleach water and persuaded Lady to set a foot in it. Then she stepped back to examine her work. Lady actually was coming out white in the patches that Emily had scrubbed, but oh dear, there was so much left to do. And the tail. How would she ever bleach that long muddy tail? She could not hold a bucket full of water high enough to soak the tail for fifteen minutes. Neither could she coax Lady to sit on the bucket while her tail bleached. Emily went back to her rubbing and scrubbing, still worrying about that tail. It was the most important part of all. A snow-white steed had to have a beautiful flowing white tail.

Emily grew more and more weary. She had been swatted several times by Lady's tail. Her arms ached. Her hands were so white and puckered they looked like corduroy. Her dress was wet and bleached in spots. Lady was *such* a big horse, and the whiter Lady became, the worse her tail looked.

Emily had bleached the easiest parts and was just finishing up under the belly—fortunately Lady did not seem to be ticklish—when she heard someone whistling a tune, and Pete Ginty appeared from behind the barn with his gun in the crook of his arm.

Now the last person in the world Emily wanted to see while Cloroxing a horse was Pete Ginty. She always felt a little timid when he was around. His eyes were so piercing and his beard, the only black beard in Pitchfork, so bushy. Everybody knew he did not believe in God. It was no wonder he was a bachelor. He had a way of talking that made Emily think he was joking, but she could never be sure, and so whenever he cut across the Bartlett property to hunt rabbits or China pheasants she stayed out of his way. Mama said she wished Pete Ginty would go hunt China pheasants in someone else's fields, but Daddy said, Oh well, he and Pete had gone to school together.

There was no time for Emily to run and hide. Pete Ginty sauntered over and stood watching her rub and scrub. Emily could feel herself turning red. She wished he would stay in his carpenter shop instead of tramping around the countryside hunting on other people's property.

Pete Ginty pushed his sweat-stained hat back on his head. "Emily," he said at last, "what the Sam Hill are you doing under that horse?"

Emily came out and stood up. "Cloroxing

it," she answered. What else could she say?

"Well, I'll be gol-dinged," said Pete Ginty. "Cloroxing a horse! I always did say women were too neat and tidy for their own good, but this beats anything I ever heard."

Emily wished Pete Ginty would go on about his business and leave her alone. "I'm *not* doing it to be neat and tidy," said Emily hotly. She was so tired and damp and smelled so strong of bleach and wet horse that she was at the point of tears. "I'm doing it because my cousin Muriel is coming out from Port-land and she has been reading a book about a beautiful black horse and I want to turn Lady into a beautiful white horse." She could hear him telling the men who hung around the livery stable about it. From now on every man she met would say, "Hello there, Emily. Cloroxed any horses lately?" Unless they said, "Fed any rotten apples to the hogs lately?" That was the trouble with a small town. Nobody could ever live any-thing down.

"Just like a woman," observed Pete Ginty.

Emily did not think he meant this to be a compliment, but she was flattered that he said woman instead of little girl.

"How are you going to do the tail?" he asked curiously.

"I don't know," confessed Emily wearily. "It's supposed to soak fifteen minutes."

Pete Ginty leaned his gun against the watering trough. "Here, give me that bucket," he ordered, and there was nothing for Emily to do but hand it over. He held the bucket under Lady's tail and lifted it so that the long hair floated in the water.

Emily was very grateful for this unexpected assistance, but her gratitude did not help her make conversation with the man who, she was certain, was going to make a good story out of this. Mama always said, "That Pete Ginty and his yarns!"

Even Pete Ginty could not hold up a bucket of water for fifteen minutes. He rested his arms several times, but when the fifteen minutes were up Lady's tail was white.

"Oh, thank you, Mr. Ginty," said Emily. "I never could have done the tail alone."

Pete Ginty was not polite enough to tell her she was welcome. He picked up his gun, snorted, "Women!" and stomped off.

Exhausted, Emily leaned against the watering trough to look at her work. Lady was now a white horse. Against the setting sun, late on a May afternoon, it seemed to Emily that Lady really was a beautiful white steed with a flowing mane and tail. She was now good enough for Muriel, and Emily could hardly wait to show her off. She did hope, however, that Muriel would not be so delighted with Lady that she would want to skip the trip to the cemetery. Emily longed for a ride in Uncle Ben's Maxwell.

"My goodness, Emily!" exclaimed Mama, when Emily had led Lady into her stall and returned to the house. "Just look at you. Dirt from head to foot." She went into the bathroom, which was just off the kitchen, and began to run water into the second bathtub in Yamhill County.

"But Mama," said Emily, "I turned Lady into a beautiful snow-white steed."

Mama smiled lovingly at Emily while the water splashed into the tub. "Beauty is in the eye of the beholder," she said.

"What does that mean?" asked Emily.

"It means that the beauty is in your mind," answered Mama with a smile, "rather than in what you see."

The funny things grown-ups said!

The next morning was a busy one. After breakfast Emily plucked the pin feathers out of the chickens Mama was going to fry for dinner. Then she helped gather lilacs to take to the cemetery to put on the graves of the pioneer ancestors. It was such a beauti-ful day for a trip out in the country, where the orchards in bloom would be as lovely as the bolts of veiling in Grandma's millinery store.

When at last Mama had no more chores for her, Emily picked trailing vines of wild sweet peas that bloomed beside the privet hedge. How beautiful the soft green leaves and purply-red blossoms would look around the neck of a snow-white steed!

When Emily entered the barn Lady nickered softly. Emily patted her flank and persuaded her to back out of her stall to be admired in the sunlight by the door. Emily twined the sweet peas into a garland around her neck and stood back to admire Lady.

But in the morning sunlight, golden with dancing motes, Emily's horse was no longer a steed. She was not even snow-white. She was an elderly plow horse, cleaner than most, with some ragged-looking pea vines around her neck. Emily wondered why she had ever seen Lady as anything else. She did not know when she had been so disappointed—not since that time at the State Fair when Daddy bought her a longed-for cone of spun sugar as fluffy and pink as a cloud in a sunset and when she bit into it, so certain that it would taste of heaven, it turned out to be a mouthful of nothing, sweet, sticky nothing. Now the morning sunlight had dissolved another dream. She should have said whoa to her imagination before it ran away with her.

Silently Emily led Lady back to her stall. Then she walked slowly back to the house. Mama was right. The beauty had not been in the horse at all. It had been in Emily's mind. She had wanted Lady to be beautiful so much that for a little while she had actually seemed beautiful.

"Why, what's the matter, Emily?" Mama looked concerned.

"Mama, today Lady is not a snow-white steed," said Emily sadly. "She is just an extra-clean plow horse. I guess the beauty went out of my eye overnight."

Mama smiled tenderly at Emily. "We all have to come down to earth sometime, Emily."

"But I don't want to disappoint Muriel," said Emily.

"I wouldn't worry about Muriel," advised Mama.

But Emily did worry about Muriel, her city cousin who knew all about horses from reading *Black Beauty* and who wrote letters on stationery instead of tablet paper.

At last the sound of Uncle Ben's automobile was heard coming down the road to the farm, and Emily ran out to greet her city relatives. She kissed Uncle Ben and Aunt Irene and said shyly, "Hello, Muriel." Muriel looked so grand with her curls, each one a long tube of shining hair.

"Hello, Emily." Muriel jumped down from the running board. "Did you get my letter?"

"Yes," said Emily. "We are going to have

a library here in Pitchfork and maybe we will have *Black Beauty* too."

"It's such a good book," said Muriel with a sigh. "It's the best book I ever read. The horse tells the story of his life."

"A horse *talks*?" Emily was incredulous. What kind of a book was this *Black Beauty*?

"Oh, yes!" said Muriel. "All the horses talk. They tell each other all their troubles."

Emily simply could not imagine what this book was like. The way Muriel spoke, the horses sounded as chatty as the ladies of Pitchfork.

Mama came running out to greet the city relatives. "You certainly picked a beautiful day," she said, when another round of kisses had been exchanged, "but you must be tired after driving all the way out from Portland."

"Mama," whispered Muriel to her mother.

Aunt Irene smiled. "Muriel wants to know

if she can go horseback riding. She has been dying to and I hope she gets it out of her system."

"Of course, dear," Mama said to Muriel, who looked embarrassed by her mother's remark. "Emily, take Muriel for a ride on Lady."

Emily was grateful to Mama for not saying she had Cloroxed Lady. "Come on, Muriel," she said, still shy in the presence of her city relatives. She wished she had taken the sweet-pea vines off Lady's neck. By this time they must be wilted, and would look more ridiculous than ever. "Suppose you wait here," she suggested, when they came to the watering trough. "I'll bring Lady out." She ran into the barn, where she discovered Lady had nibbled at the pea vines until only a few blossoms were left on the floor of the stall. As she led Lady down the ramp from the barn she was about to say apologetically, "She's just an old plow horse," when she happened to glance at Muriel's face.

"A white horse!" exclaimed Muriel, her face alight with admiration. "That's even better than a black horse."

Well! Emily was encouraged. Why bother to tell Muriel that Lady was just an old plow horse? Mama was right. Beauty was in the eye of the beholder. There it was, shining out of Muriel's eye as plain as plain could be.

Lady tossed her head and whinnied. Looking frightened, Muriel drew back, encouraging Emily even more. Muriel not only couldn't tell a plow horse when she saw one, she was also scared of it. "Easy there, girl," Emily said to Lady, with mounting confidence. "Muriel, if you just climb up on the edge of the watering trough you can mount Lady."

"Shouldn't—shouldn't the horse have a saddle?" Muriel asked.

"I never use one," answered Emily and noted that her cousin was impressed. Her spirits rose even higher as she persuaded Lady to stand beside the watering trough. "Climb on," she said to her cousin.

"It—it won't run away or anything?" Muriel asked timidly. "In *Black Beauty* horses sometimes ran away."

"I don't think so," answered Emily truthfully.

"Well—here goes." Muriel grasped Lady's mane and threw her leg over the horse's broad back. Her bloomers showed, but it did not matter. There were no boys around. "I—I didn't know a horse was so slippery."

Emily began to lead Lady around the barnyard. The horse plodded patiently along, but Muriel kept both hands tightly clutched on the mane. She managed to look both delighted and terrified at the same time.

Lady switched her tail and flicked Muriel's leg.

"Emily!" cried Muriel in fright.

"It's all right," Emily assured her. "She's just brushing off a fly."

Around and around the barnyard they went. Muriel began to gain confidence. She sat up straighter and her knuckles were no longer white from her tight grip on the mane. "You don't think the horse will get tired, do you?" she asked.

"No." Emily did not tell her cousin that Lady was used to pulling a plow for hours at a time.

"In *Black Beauty* some of the masters were terribly cruel to horses," said Muriel. "I wouldn't want to be cruel to a horse."

Emily could hardly keep from giggling. A walk around the barnyard cruel to Lady! She began to wonder if Muriel would never get tired. She did not want to miss the ride out to the cemetery in Uncle Ben's Maxwell.

Around and around they went. It must be almost time for the rest of the family to leave. Muriel looked as if she planned to stick to that horse forever.

"Would you like to go faster?" Emily asked suddenly.

"Oh yes," agreed Muriel confidently.

"Giddyap!" cried Emily, and pulling on the rope, began to run.

Obediently Lady broke into a heavy trot. Muriel began to bounce. Lady's broad back was slippery and Muriel bounced to one side and then to the other. "You're going—too—fast." The words were jarred out of her.

Emily pretended not to hear. Clomp, clomp, clomp went Lady's big hoofs. Slap, slap, slap went Muriel. Her curls were bouncing up and down like springs.

"Heh–heh–help!" said Muriel breath-lessly.

"Whoa!" cried Emily, and slowed to a walk.

"Girls!" called Aunt Irene from the back porch. "We're going now. Do you want to come along?"

"We're coming," called Emily, because Muriel was too out of breath to answer. She led Lady back to the watering trough and helped Muriel dismount. "You do want to go, don't you, Muriel?" she asked.

Muriel nodded, and Emily led Lady through the gate into the pasture, where she removed her halter and gave her a fare-well pat.

"Shouldn't you put a cloth over her?" asked Muriel, who had caught her breath.

"A cloth?" Emily was puzzled. "What for?"

"Well, in *Black Beauty* whenever a horse

had a lot of exercise the groom put a cloth over its back," Muriel explained. She added dreamily, "Sometimes the groom even gave the horse some nice warm mash."

Emily did not like to bring her cousin down to earth by telling her that Lady had not had any real exercise. "It's such a warm sunny day Lady doesn't need a cloth," she said tactfully, "and she likes nice juicy grass better than mash."

This satisfied Muriel. "You can ride some more when we come back," offered Emily, as the cousins ran off to join their parents. "I'll lead you again."

"Oh, would you?" exclaimed Muriel gratefully.

"Did you have a nice ride?" asked Aunt Irene, when the girls reached the automobile.

"Oh, Mama, it was just wonderful!" said Muriel. "Just think, I have really ridden a horse. A beautiful white horse!"

Mama and Emily exchanged a little smile. They both knew where the beauty was. Then Emily climbed up into the back seat of Uncle Ben's Maxwell and sat down on the shiny leather cushion. She admired the little vases for flowers and the plaid auto robe hanging on the back of the front seat. She gave a little bounce and discovered that the cushion was springy, which pleased her very much. The road out to the cemetery was good and bumpy.

4
Grandpa
and The Tin Lizzie

Grandpa's mind was made up. He was going to buy an automobile! Yes, Grandpa said, times were changing. Horse-and-buggy days were at an end. He wanted to keep up with the times and so he was going to buy a Ford, a Model T Ford.

Emily thought this was terribly exciting— Grandpa keeping up with the times in a new automobile. She had always thought Grandpa was pretty old-fashioned even if he did not wear a beard. Why, he still called electricity "juice." "Switch off the light," he would say. "We don't want to waste the juice." But now Grandpa was going to change his ways, and Emily was going to be closely related to an automobile. When the boys and girls at school bragged about their families' automobiles, Emily had always said proudly, "We don't have an automobile. *We* have a tractor."

It seemed as if everyone had a different opinion about Grandpa's buying an automobile. Grandma could not see why he wanted such a contraption. My land, a person could walk any place he wanted to go in Pitchfork and when was he going to find time to drive, with the store open until all hours? Mama said she did hope he wouldn't do anything reckless at his age. Daddy just laughed and said let him have his fun.

Grandpa's customers joshed him about his

plans to buy an automobile. Every morning the old men who came in to sit around the store, while they waited for Uncle Avery to sort the morning mail, asked, "Well, Will, have you bought that Tin Lizzie yet?"

Emily was on pins and needles for fear Grandpa might change his mind about keeping up with the times, but at last the great day came. Mama and Emily went uptown to help Grandma mind the store while Grandpa took the new auto stage to McMinnville to buy the Model T Ford.

Emily practiced trying to shake open a paper bag with a flourish and a snap, the way Grandpa did, so that people would look at her with admiration and say, "The way that girl snaps paper bags!" While she tried and tried, Grandma fussed and worried and declared it was foolishness for Grandpa to drive back from McMinnville in that contraption when he had never driven before.

Late in the afternoon Mama kept going out on the porch and peering down Main Street in the direction of McMinnville. Emily could not see what they were worried about. What was there to driving an automobile besides starting, stopping and, in a pinch, backing up? Old George A. Barbee had explained it all to Grandpa before he left that morning. There was nothing to it except sometimes on a steep hill it was necessary to turn around and back up the hill so the gasoline could run down into the engine.

"Mercy!" Grandma would exclaim, going out to peer down Main Street. "I hope he hasn't hit a cow the way old George A. did that time."

It was Emily, tired of trying to shake open paper bags, who went out to sit on the front steps and saw Grandpa driving down the road as nice as you please. "He's coming!"

she shouted. "He's coming!"

Mama, Grandma, and all the customers rushed out to the sidewalk to watch Grandpa's arrival. There he came, down the road and across the bridge and up Main Street. Beaming and triumphant, he drew up in front of his store. "Whoa!" he cried as he stopped his new automobile.

"William, you made it!" exclaimed Grandma in relief.

"Of course I made it," answered Grandpa, climbing over the door on the driver's side, which was not made to be opened.

Everyone clustered around to inspect and admire Grandpa's new black touring car. Old George A. Barbee was there to open the hood and inspect the engine. Old George A., as everyone in Pitchfork called him, was the town's authority on Fords, because he had been the first to own one.

Emily was a little disappointed because

the Ford did not have a vase for flowers on the dashboard, but it did have a number of features that made up for it—the little brass radiator ornament, and the red, white, and blue cans for extra water, gas, and oil that were mounted on the running board. Because Emily was related to the car, she felt free to climb into the front seat and bounce up and down on the black leather cushion.

"Come along, Emily," said Mama. "It's time to go home and fix supper."

"Mama!" protested Emily. "I want to go for a ride."

"Not today," said Mama firmly. "Come along."

"I'll drive you home," offered Grandpa.

"No, thank you," answered Mama. "There are too many customers for Mother to handle alone. Come *along*, Emily."

Bitterly disappointed, Emily climbed out of the car. "But Mama," protested Emily, as they turned off the cement sidewalk onto the boardwalk. "I've been waiting all day to ride in Grandpa's Model T."

"Now, Emily," said Mama firmly. "You are not to set foot in that automobile for a good long time. I just don't trust your grandfather's driving."

"Mama!" wailed Emily.

And so, as the days went by, Emily's mother made up excuses to keep Emily out of her grandfather's automobile, and Emily watched wistfully as he rattled around town, keeping up with the times.

Grandpa was not the only person keeping up with the times. The Ladies' Civic Club had found space for a library in a corner of the Commercial Clubrooms upstairs over the Pitchfork State Bank. Two ladies loaned old china closets, with glass doors that could be locked, to be used for book shelves. Mama was appointed librarian. Now all they needed was books.

Mama wrote a letter which was published on the front page of the *Pitchfork Report*. She asked anyone who had a book to give to the library to leave it in a box in Grandpa's store. She also asked anyone about to subscribe to the *Country Gentleman* at one dollar a year to telephone her. If the library could get five subscriptions, it would receive five new books absolutely free. The seventy-five books loaned by the state library would arrive any day now.

Then one Sunday, when the store was closed and no one had banged on the door to get Grandpa to open up, Grandpa and Grandma drove over to the farm in the new Ford. Grandma was wearing her good serge suit and her best hat. She had a resigned do-or-die look on her gentle face.

"Come on," said Grandpa. "We've come to take the whole family for a ride."

"Good," said Daddy. "I've been itching to go for a ride."

This time there was no way out for Mama. Emily and her mother and father climbed into the back seat. Grandpa got out and cranked the car—and cranked it and cranked it. Finally the engine started, with a noise like machinery sneezing, and the automobile began to shimmy. Grandpa ran around and climbed in fast and off they drove, trailing two brown veils of dust behind them. Fong Quock, who was out tending his vegetable garden, shouted and waved. Grandpa honked his horn in reply—*a-ooga, a-ooga*.

"Mercy!" exclaimed Grandma, as Grandpa whizzed around the corner onto Main Street. *A-ooga, a-ooga*. Grandpa honked at a boy on a bicycle. Mama looked nervous. Daddy beamed. Emily waved to everyone she saw. What a ride they had! Down Main Street, past the school, down an unpaved road trailing dust and scattering chickens, up Depot Road, around to Main Street, back up the road to the farm. They had not had a single accident; they had not hit a cow or even a chicken!

"Say, Emily," said Grandpa, before he and Grandma drove off, "how would you like to drive out to the old Skinner place with me in the morning?" The old Skinner place was a piece of land which Grandpa owned and which was farmed for him by a nearby farmer. Several people had owned it since the Skinners had sold it back around 1890, but in Pitchfork land was almost always called after the name of the pioneer who had taken up the donation land claim.

"Oh, Grandpa, I would love to," answered Emily quickly.

Mama hesitated before she said, "Mrs. Scott phoned to say she had some books to give to the library but no way to get into town. Perhaps you could stop at the Scott place and pick them up."

It was all right. At last Emily was free to ride in Grandpa's Ford and keep up with the times, too.

The next morning, bright and early, Grandpa drove up to the farm for Emily, who was waiting for him on the gate out by the catalpa tree. This was going to be even better than Emily had hoped, because Grandpa had put down the top of his car. Mama, still looking worried, came out on the porch to wave good-bye.

Unfortunately, Emily and Grandpa had to pass old George A. Barbee's house on the way out of town. When the old gentleman heard them approaching he crawled out from under his own Model T Ford and hailed them. Naturally Grandpa had to stop, although he did not turn off the engine. Old George A. came over and leaned against Grandpa's automobile. Emily could see he had settled down for a good long talk about the insides of Fords. Emily squirmed around on the leather seat while the two old men discussed such tiresome things as spindle-joint anti-rattlers, slipping clutches, low bands that might burn out, the advantages of a Ruxtell axle. . . . It seemed to her that the chugging motor was as eager to be off as she was.

Finally Emily simply could not stand it. "Grandpa," she said urgently above the noise of the engine, "don't you think we'd better go?"

"Yes, Emily, I expect we'd better," agreed Grandpa. "Well, thanks for the advice, George A."

At last they were on their way! It was a beautiful day for a drive in the country in an automobile with the top down. The fields were green; the sky was blue with whipped-cream clouds; wild roses and Queen Anne's lace bloomed along the fences. Blackbirds glistened in the sun. If Grandpa's automobile had not been making so much noise they could have heard the meadowlarks.

The road was good and bumpy, and Emily enjoyed every bump they hit. "Can you go faster, Grandpa?" she asked.

Grandpa pulled down the gas lever on the steering wheel. The Ford leaped ahead. Emily jounced and bounced around on the leather seat, but she managed to look at the needle on the speedometer which Grandpa had had installed. "Grandpa!" she shrieked. "We're going twenty-five miles an hour!" The joy and the wonder of it! Tearing along at twenty-five miles an hour.

They stopped under the old maple in front of the Scott place while Mrs. Scott ran out with her books for the library. Emily was much disappointed, although she was careful not to let Mrs. Scott, a tired, wispy little woman, know it. There were only three books, all of them very old, with yellowed paper and fine print. *Kenilworth* and two books of sermons. No *Black Beauty*. Emily thanked her. It was nice of her to give her books, the only books she had.

Farther out in the country the wagon road

to the old Skinner place wound through several farms and at each farm Grandpa had to stop and climb out over the door. He opened the gate, climbed back into his Ford, drove through, got out and closed the gate, climbed back in, and drove on to the next gate. The first section of the road led them through a barnyard, where Grandpa had to swerve to avoid some chickens and a calf.

Finally they reached the old Skinner place. How quiet it was with the engine of Grandpa's car turned off! Grandpa climbed out to examine his alfalfa crop while Emily picked a bouquet of wild columbine growing along the fence, to take home to Mama.

"Come on, Emily," Grandpa called at last. "Time to go. I don't like to leave your grandmother alone with the store all morning."

Emily started to climb up on the running board with her bouquet of columbine when she heard a sound. At first she thought it was a tractor, but then she realized it was not. It was an airplane! "Look, Grandpa!" she cried, pointing. "An airplane!"

"By George, you're right!" exclaimed Grandpa, shading his eyes with his hand.

"Grandpa, I can see the aviator!" cried Emily ecstatically. And she could! She could see his brown leather jacket and helmet and even his goggles. What an exciting morning this was! She waved frantically. The man in the airplane waved to her over the side of the cockpit. It was almost too much to bear. She had been waved at by an aviator! "Grandpa, he waved!" Emily could hardly believe it. She stood watching until the airplane disappeared in the distance. Then she climbed into the Ford and slammed the door. The things she had to tell Mama!

Emily and her grandfather were not even

near the first gate when Grandpa began to work the clutch pedal up and down. It seemed lifeless under his foot.

"Grandpa!" Emily was alarmed.

"Great Scott!" Grandpa was alarmed, too. "Now what the Sam Hill was it old George A. said to do in a case like this?" He pumped the clutch once more before it came to him. "He said if this ever happened I'd better not stop, because I couldn't get started again unless I was on a hill."

"Then don't stop," begged Emily. Right here all the hills were in the distance, where they could do no good.

"We're coming to the gate!" yelled Grandpa.

"You can't stop!" shouted Emily. The gate seemed to be flying toward her. "Grandpa, don't stop!"

"I've got to!" yelled Grandpa.

"No!" shrieked Emily. "We'll never

get home." My goodness, if she didn't get home, Mama would worry and she would never get to go for a ride again. Just when Emily thought they were going to crash into the gate, Grandpa turned aside and his automobile went bounding around in his alfalfa crop. Grandpa drove around and around in a circle. "It's no use, Emily," he said. "I'll have to stop. There's nothing else to do. We can hike to the nearest farm and get a farmer with a team to tow us back to town."

"No, wait, Grandpa," begged Emily. Be towed back to town behind old-fashioned horses? I should say not! Grandpa and his wonderful new automobile would be the laughingstock of Pitchfork. Besides, it would take all morning or longer, and Emily was very anxious not to worry Mama. "If you drive real slow," she suggested, "I could jump out and open the gate."

"Emily, you might get hurt," protested Grandpa.

"No, I won't," Emily assured him. "I'll be careful."

"I guess I could see how slow I can drive." Grandpa sounded dubious, but he was not eager to be towed back by horses either. He was proud of his Ford and wanted to ride back in style. They slowed down until they were bouncing gently over the ruts. Emily held her breath for fear the engine might stop altogether and there they would be, out in the middle of an alfalfa field, miles from nowhere.

"You're sure you can do it?" asked Grandpa.

"I'm sure." Emily laid her bouquet of columbine on the seat. She opened the door and looked down. The ground was passing by faster than she had expected. She took a deep breath and jumped. She stumbled and fell, skinning her knee. Never mind. It was half-sock weather and her knee would heal. "I'm all right," she called out, and while Grandpa speeded up and went on driving in circles through the alfalfa, she ran to the gate, climbed up and lifted off the ring of wire that secured it to the fence post. She pushed off with one foot and riding the gate,

she swung out across the road. If she had not been so worried it would have been fun. Swinging on gates was forbidden at home.

Grandpa drove through the gate and started going around in circles in the next field. Emily hopped off the gate before the dust had settled and pushed and shoved until it was closed once more. She slipped the circle of wire back in place and ran after the Ford. She had worked fast, because this field of wheat did not belong to Grandpa and the farmer who owned it might not like Grandpa driving around on his crop. Emily was glad it was a field of wheat and not a prune orchard. Grandpa would have had a terrible time if he had to drive in circles through an orchard.

Grandpa slowed down until Emily was afraid the engine would stop. She grabbed the edge of the Ford beside the seat cushion and pulled herself up on the running board.

Then she flopped into the seat. Whew! She had made it!

"Good work, Emily," said Grandpa, and drove in a straight line down the wagon road once more.

Emily leaned back and concentrated on catching her breath before the next gate. If she had done it once she could do it again. She had to or be towed back by horses.

At the second gate Grandpa began to circle once more. Emily opened the door, for an instant glad that Mama could not see her now, and leaped bravely through the air. She stumbled again but managed not to fall. She must be getting the hang of it. Once more she slipped off the wire hoop. This gate creaked and Emily could not ride it. She had to shove. Grandpa straightened out his driving and went through. Emily tried not to breathe dust while she struggled to close the gate, and Grandpa circled through the oats until she could scramble aboard. Whew! That was hard work. Emily hoped she had enough strength left for the third and last gate.

That gate was in view of some farm buildings. Grandpa circled slowly. Emily took a deep breath and leaped. Yes, she did seem to have the hang of it, because she landed on her feet. She ran to the gate, unfastened it, and tried to pull it open. It still would not budge. Desperately Emily shoved. What if Grandpa ran out of gas while he was circling around!

"Can you lift it up, Emily?" Grandpa yelled, as he drove past.

Emily lifted. The gate budged but that was all. Emily lifted again and managed to get the gate partway open but not enough for an automobile to pass through. She wondered if it would be too selfish to ask God to help her in this one little thing. "Don't stop, Grandpa," she begged. "I'll think of something."

An inquisitive calf came bounding across the barnyard to see what was going on. It would be dreadful if he got through the gate. Emily would never be able to catch him in that big field and Grandpa really would run out of gas while she tried. She put one hand on the gatepost and the other on the gate. The calf frolicked over and nuzzled her with his moist nose. "Shoo!" she cried. "Go away!"

The farmer came out of the barn with a pitchfork in his hands. "What the Sam Hill is going on here?" he yelled, dropping the pitchfork and running toward Emily.

"Don't stop, Grandpa," pleaded Emily, as the calf licked her face with his long, wet tongue. "I'll ask the man to open the gate."

"What are you driving around in my oats for?" demanded the farmer.

"I can't stop," yelled Grandpa. "I'll never get her started again."

"Please open the gate for us," begged Emily, shoving at the calf with her foot. If only the farmer would help them out!

The farmer began to laugh. "Beat it, Buttercup," he said, slapping the calf on the rump. Then he opened the gate for Emily.

"Oh, thank you," said Emily, with great feeling. "Thank you ever so much." She hoped she was doing a good job of thanking the farmer. If Grandpa felt he had to thank him too, he might think he had to stop. No, it was all right. Grandpa was circling the barnyard, skillfully avoiding three chickens and the bounding Buttercup.

The farmer stood watching Emily with something like admiration as she leaped to the running board when Grandpa drove by.

"Thank you," she called again, to make sure, as she flopped into the seat.

"Thank you, sir," Grandpa yelled above the noise of the engine.

"You're welcome," the farmer yelled back. "Next time get a horse!"

Gracious! Emily hoped the farmer did not get to town often. She did not want this adventure to get around Pitchfork. Grandpa would never hear the last of it and Mama might not let her go driving again.

"Yes sir, Emily," said Grandpa, as they headed back toward Pitchfork, "I always said you were a humdinger."

The ride back to town was peaceful enough, although Emily was a little nervous lest they meet a cow in the middle of the road that might force them to stop. It would be awful if they had to stop now after all she had been through. When they came to Main Street, she said, "I can walk home from the store, Grandpa, as easy as not."

"All right, Emily," agreed Grandpa. "You

know, I have a feeling your mother might not think too highly of what went on this morning. Probably I shouldn't have let you do it. Maybe we had better keep it a secret, you and me."

"Yes, let's," agreed Emily, who was happy that Grandpa wasn't going to tell, either. Secrets were fun and she was pleased that she and Grandpa had one all their own to share.

"Whoa!" cried Grandpa, stopping in front of the store just as if there was nothing wrong with his Model T. Old George A. Barbee would be only too happy to tell him how to fix it.

When Emily climbed out with Mrs. Scott's three books and the bouquet of columbine, she discovered her legs felt wobbly. "Thank you for the ride, Grandpa," she said, not feeling the least bit like a humdinger.

Grandpa's eyes twinkled. "Thank *you*, Emily. I don't know what I'd have done without you." He meant it, too.

Emily walked home on shaky legs. No running or skipping this morning. She found Mama on the back porch doing the washing, which seemed surprising until Emily realized that it was only mid-morning even though she felt as if she had been gone a long, long time.

"What lovely columbine!" Mama smiled over the wringer. "Did you have a nice ride, Emily?"

"Yes, Mama." Wearily Emily sat down on the back steps to rest. "But Mama, I don't think many people will want to read Mrs. Scott's donation."

"Oh, that's too bad." Mama folded a pair of overalls so they would go through the wringer.

"And Mama," said Emily, "the most exciting thing happened. I was waved at by an aviator! An airplane flew over and I waved at him and he waved back."

"Why Emily, that's the second airplane that has been around here this year!" Mama guided the overalls into a washtub of rinse water. "Just think, it was only about seventy-five years ago that your pioneer ancestors came here by covered wagon, and now your grandfather is driving his automobile and airplanes are flying over!" She fished another pair of overalls from the suds in the washing machine. "Emily, your grandfather is right. Times are changing and he is right to keep up with them, even at his age."

As Emily bent over to examine her skinned knee, she could not help thinking that it had been all she could do to keep up with Grandpa's Tin Lizzie.

5

A Tarnished Silver Dollar

Summer was a busy time on the farm. Mama and Emily canned fruits and vegetables, jars and jars of fruits and vegetables. Emily snapped the beans and slipped the skins off so many peaches that she began to feel as if the skin was about to slip off her hands. Mama even found time to can pie cherries, and Emily became expert at flipping pits out of cherries with a buttonhook.

All day long the wash boiler full of jars

steamed and bubbled on top of the stove, but in the middle of every morning and every afternoon Emily escaped from the hot kitchen to take a Mason jar of lemonade without sugar to Daddy, who was working in the fields. Daddy, his denim shirt soaked and his sunburned face streaming with sweat, was mighty glad to see Emily and that jar of lemonade. On the way back to the house Emily always wanted to pick a bouquet of bachelor's buttons, but she never did. When Daddy was her age, all the Bartlett boys had to work long hours weeding bachelor's buttons out of the fields and to this day Daddy did not want to see the pesky things in a vase in the house. It was too bad, because Emily dearly loved to gather wildflowers.

Summer was such a busy time that Emily was afraid Mama and the Ladies' Civic Club might forget about the library. She should have known Mama would not forget something once she had started it. Every week Mama managed to find time to send some news about the library to the *Pitchfork Report*. Sixty-two books had been given to the library. (Mama did not put in the paper that the sixty-two books were not very good books. She did not want to discourage people from giving.) More books were needed, especially books for boys and girls. Another bookcase or cupboard with doors that could be locked would be useful. Any plans for raising money for shelves and books would be gratefully received. And finally the important announcement— the library was actually going to open on Saturday afternoon in the Commercial Club-rooms, upstairs over the Pitchfork State Bank, and a gala occasion it was going to be. The whole town was invited and there was to be a silver tea. People could borrow books and keep them for two weeks. It was going to be a big day in Pitchfork.

"Mama, what's a silver tea?" asked Emily, thinking that it sounded very special, like a golden wedding.

"A way of raising money," answered Mama. "We will put a plate on the tea table, and everyone who can will leave a silver coin on it to help the library."

Silver coins could mean silver dollars or it could mean ten-cent pieces. Emily hoped for silver dollars, lots of them, because someday Mama hoped Pitchfork would have a real library in a room by itself, with an encyclopedia and open shelves full of books.

Emily could hardly wait for Saturday to come. During the week the stationmaster at the depot telephoned Mama to say that a crate of books had arrived from the state library. Mama had Grandpa pick up the crate in his Ford and deliver it to the Commercial Clubrooms. And wouldn't you know?

That was the week the tomatoes were ripe and Mama was so busy canning tomatoes and selling tomatoes to other ladies who wanted to can them that she did not have time to go uptown and open that crate. Emily could hardly stand it, she was so anxious to find out if the state library had sent *Black Beauty*, that book about the chatty horses she was so curious to read. Or maybe—terrible thought—the state library in Salem, capital of Oregon, was so big and so grand it would not bother to send books to boys and girls. Maybe it had more important things to do.

Finally Saturday actually did arrive and Mama decided they had so much to do to get ready for the tea they would just stack the dinner dishes in the sink. Mama put on her best gray silk dress, and Emily wore the scratchy yellow organdy that Grandma had made for her. The only thing in the world that scratched as much as an organdy dress was a slide in a straw stack, but today Emily did not care if the organdy did scratch. She wanted to look her best for the silver tea. Mama gave her ten cents to tie in the corner of her handkerchief until she could drop it on the plate on the tea table.

When Emily and her mother climbed the steep stairs to the Commercial Clubrooms they found the members of the Ladies' Civic Club flying around getting ready for the tea. The table was already set with someone's best white linen tablecloth and a glass basket of pink cosmos had been placed in the center. Cookies and tiny sandwiches were laid out on plates. The table really did look very pretty even though the room smelled of stale cigar smoke and was furnished with cuspidors and leather chairs with the stuffing coming out. In one corner, over by the old china closets someone had loaned to be used as bookcases, was the crate from the state library.

"Mama," whispered Emily. "When are

you going to open the crate?"

"Now Emily," said Mama firmly, "just remember that no one is to take books until after I give my talk. And remember, too, that you are the librarian's daughter. You can choose just one book. It would not look right for you to take more."

"Just one, Mama?"

"Just one."

One book was better than no books, thought Emily, and next week she could change it. Just let that one book be *Black Beauty* was all she hoped.

"Let's open some windows and air this place out," said Mrs. Archer.

People began to climb the stairs to the clubrooms. Soon the room was abloom with some of Grandma's prettiest hats, although not all the ladies wore hats. Many farm women who were in town to do their week's shopping wore cotton housedresses and no hats at all. Arlene Twitchell, the prettiest girl in town, arrived with some music in her hand, and Mrs. Warty Thompson opened the piano.

"Mama, she isn't going to sing, is she?" whispered Emily, who was anxious to get on with the opening of the library and knew that Arlene never stopped with one song.

"Shh. Yes," answered Mama.

Then someone discovered that no one had brought any sugar cubes, and Emily was sent off to Grandpa's store to fetch some. By the time she returned, folding chairs had been set up and Mama had unpacked the crate and set the state books on the shelves. Emily edged over toward the china cupboards.

Mama fumbled in her handbag and brought out a fifty-cent piece. "Here, Emily," she whispered. "Put this on that empty plate along with your dime. If people see some silver on the plate, they will be more apt to donate to the library."

After Emily did as she was told, Mrs. Warty Thompson sat down at the piano and Arlene Twitchell began to sing. She sang *Ah, Sweet Mystery of Life* and *I'm Forever Blowing Bubbles*. Emily was careful to clap just hard enough to be polite but not hard enough to encourage her to sing a third song. Arlene did look so pretty with her dark curly hair and her white dotted Swiss dress.

"My, just look at the work her mother put on that dress," Emily heard someone whisper.

"It's no wonder she is spoiled," was the whispered answer. "I feel sorry for the man who marries her."

Emily could not help thinking how pleasant it would be to have curly hair and be spoiled. Then Mrs. George Thompson played *Humoresque* on the violin. Everybody in town had heard Mrs. Thompson play

Humoresque dozens of times, but a violin solo did make the tea seem more stylish. Besides, everybody in town liked Mrs. George Thompson. No one had ever heard her say an unkind word about anybody.

More people kept coming, including some of the men of the town, who said they wanted to have a look at this library. They stayed to eat and joke about the tiny sandwiches. And then—oh, dear—who should arrive but Fong Quock! Emily hoped he would not notice her in the crowd. She squeezed toward the back of the room, where he would not see her.

Mama gave a little talk about how she hoped someday the library could have a room of its own with open shelves (instead of somebody's old china closets, thought Emily) and what a valuable thing an encyclopedia would be for the town. It occurred to Emily that even though her hair was not curly and she could never hope to grow up to be the prettiest girl in town, she was still one of the most important girls in Pitchfork. She was the daughter of the librarian, the niece of the mayor, and the only girl in town who could go behind the counters in Grandpa's store. She was also the girl who had licked the stamp that carried Mama's letter to the state library.

Mama finished her talk and the library of Pitchfork, Oregon, was open for business!

Tea was served and Emily was torn between getting a peek at the books and staying where she could keep an eye on the plate of silver. It turned out she had no choice. Mama asked her to pass the cream and sugar on a little tray.

"Why can't June do it?" whispered Emily, who had seen her cousin in the crowd.

"She might spill the cream," answered Mama.

"Did they send *Black Beauty*?" whispered

Emily, as she picked up the tray with the sugar bowl and cream pitcher.

"Not this time. Now don't worry. I'll save you a book if it looks as if they will all be taken." Mama went to take up her duties as librarian.

Pleased to be trusted with the cream pitcher, Emily circulated through the crowd. "Cream and sugar?" she asked politely, of anyone holding a cup of tea.

"Why, hello, Emily. How nice you look," the ladies would say. Not how pretty—how nice. "Yes, I would like a lump of sugar for my tea."

Out of the corner of her eye Emily could see her cousin June. The elastic in one of her bloomer legs was loose, and she was leaning over the tea table eating cookies and watching the plate for pieces of silver. *Plink. Plink.* It sounded as if dimes were being dropped. Emily did not hear any *plunks* that would mean someone had given a whole dollar.

Plank. That sounded like a quarter. *Plink.* *Plank.* A dime and a quarter. Every little bit helped.

Then Mrs. George Thompson served Fong Quock a cup of tea.

Oh dear, thought Emily. Now she would have to go offer him cream and sugar. She hesitated, wondering if by some lucky chance he might have forgotten about Plince.

"Emily," said Mrs. Thompson, "perhaps Mr. Quock would like some cream and sugar."

There was nothing for Emily to do but offer it to him. "Cream and sugar?" she asked, her eyes on the floor.

"No, fank you," said Fong Quock. "Missy leave Plince home today?"

"Yes, I did," mumbled Emily, sensing rather than seeing the smile on Fong Quock's face. She did not have to stand there, did she? Not when he didn't want any cream and sugar. She hurried on to another tea drinker, sloshing the cream as she went.

June must have had her fill of cookies, because she wandered over to the china closets to look over the books. Tray in hand, Emily stepped lightly over a cuspidor and made her way to the library corner. She was not going to have June beat her to the books if she could help it.

"Oh, there's Emily with the cream and sugar," said a lady. "You are just the girl I have been looking for."

Dutifully Emily held out her tray while the lady helped herself to three lumps of sugar.

"My, but you do look nice in your yellow organdy," said the lady. "Just like a little buttercup."

Emily did not feel like a little buttercup. Her organdy dress scratched around the neck and arms and she was filled with impatience.

Then *plunk*. Emily's sharp ears caught the sound of someone's dropping a whole big dollar on the plate on the table. It was—of all people—Fong Quock! The ladies near the tea table exchanged surprised glances while the old man, smiling and nodding, made his way to the stairs. Emily stared after him in astonishment. A whole silver dollar!

There were two more plunks on the plate that afternoon. Mr. Archer, the president of the bank downstairs, left a dollar, and Grandma managed to get away from the store long enough to drink a cup of tea and leave another dollar.

Three whole silver dollars, but Fong Quock's dollar was the one everybody talked about, and talk they did. "Well now, wasn't that nice of him, especially when he can read very little English himself?" "Imagine, the old fellow's taking the trouble to come up here and give a dollar to the library—I

wonder if he is lonely since he sold his confectionery store." "I have always heard that
the Chinese are scholarly people and it must

be true." "And my dear, did you see it? The dollar was actually tarnished, he has had it so long. I'll bet he still has the first dollar he ever earned." "Not now he hasn't, because he just gave it to the library." This last remark brought forth kindly laughter.

By this time everyone seemed to be well supplied with cream and sugar, so Emily set her tray on the tea table and slipped around the edge of the room to the library corner. "Mama, did you save me a book?" she asked.

"There are still books left to choose from," answered Mama.

And there were! Just think of it, real library books right here in Pitchfork, Oregon. *The Dutch Twins, The Tale of Jemima Puddleduck*—what a tiny book that was! Emily had not known they made such little books. *The Curly-haired Hen, English Fairy Tales*. But no *Black Beauty*. Oh well, perhaps another time. Emily chose *English Fairy Tales* because it was the thickest, and Mama wrote her name on a little card that she removed from a pocket in the book. Emily now had a library book to read. She could hardly wait to write to her cousin Muriel in Portland.

Emily had settled down in a slippery leather armchair to begin her book, when something made her glance toward the top of the stairs. A strange boy about Emily's age stood in the doorway. He was wearing clean faded overalls and his hair must have been cut with a pair of dull scissors by his father. He looked uncertainly at the ladies' hats and the tea table and turned to leave.

"Won't you come in?" asked Mama, with a smile.

The boy was glad to have someone welcome him. Shyly he approached Mama's table. "Ma'am, is it all right if I get some books for my family?" he asked.

Mama smiled at the boy. "I don't believe I have seen you in Pitchfork before. Do you live in the country?"

"No, ma'am. I live in Greenvale," he answered. "We read about the library in the *Pitchfork Report* and I walked down the railroad track to see if we could get some books too."

"Why, that's at least four miles," said Mama, "and four miles back again."

The boy looked at the floor. "Yes ma'am."

"Of course you may take books for your family," said Mama. This boy wanted to read. That was enough for her. It made no difference where he lived.

Emily watched while the boy, oblivious to everyone else, selected his books with care. A book about wild animals. That must be for himself. *The Tale of Jemima Puddleduck* for a little brother or sister. Two grown-up books that must be for his mother and father.

When Mama had written his name on the little cards, the boy pulled a clean white flour sack out of his hip pocket, unfolded it and carefully put the books inside. "I'll take good care of them, ma'am, and bring them back next Saturday."

"I hope you enjoy them," said Mama, watching the boy as he slipped through the crowd and disappeared down the stairs. "Just think, that boy is willing to walk eight miles along a railroad track for books," she remarked, and Emily thought that Mama looked both happy and sad at the same time.

Gradually the crowd drifted away, until at last only Emily and the members of the Ladies' Civic Club were left. The ladies gathered around the table Mama was using for a desk to watch Mama count the pieces of silver that people had given to the library. Sixteen dollars and twenty cents. It seemed like a lot of money to Emily, but Mama looked disappointed. She sighed, and said, "The people in our town just don't have much money to give to a library."

The ladies of the Civic Club said they must not be discouraged. Next time they would try a whist party. They would have a real library yet. Look at the books that had circulated that afternoon. Why, a lady way out in the country had even sent a note by a neighbor, asking for a nice cheerful book. And that boy who asked for a book on forestry, and the man who wanted a book on Oregon history. . . . Didn't this show that the people of Pitchfork really wanted a library?

"And the boy with the white flour sack," Emily whispered to Mama. "Don't forget him."

"Especially the boy with the white flour sack," agreed Mama. "For that boy we must get a library started."

And me, thought Emily. I still want

Black Beauty. She picked up Fong Quock's tarnished silver dollar. "Mama, do you suppose this really is the first dollar he ever earned?"

Mama laughed. "Oh Emily, that is just an expression. You know how people talk. I am sure it isn't his first dollar because he has been supporting his family in China all these years."

Emily was astonished. She had thought all along that Fong Quock was a bachelor like Pete Ginty. "Then what was he doing here in Pitchfork?" she asked.

"He came to Oregon to seek his fortune," said Mama, locking up the china closets even though they were almost empty of books. "Many Chinese did in the old days and somehow he found his way to Pitchfork and stayed. I can't say I blame him. It is a beautiful spot, even if the pioneers did name it Pitchfork."

To seek his fortune! Like Dick Whittington in one of the readers at school. "Do you think he found his fortune?" Emily asked doubtfully, because Pitchfork seemed to her an unlikely place to seek one's fortune. There were no streets paved with gold and no Lord Mayor, just Main Street paved in concrete, and Uncle Avery at the post office.

"I don't know," answered Mama, gathering up her handbag and the book she had chosen for herself. "Perhaps he did. He owns his little house and until he sold it not long ago he had a prosperous little business. At least he has been able to send money back to China all these years. Fortune means different things to different people, you know."

Emily hugged her book and thought this over as she and Mama descended the stairs to the sidewalk. Mama was right, she decided. Fortune did mean different things to different people. And to Emily right now, fortune meant not streets paved with gold or money to send to China. It meant the people of Pitchfork having enough money to give some to the library. Enough for real book shelves and an encyclopedia and some left over for *Black Beauty*.

6

The Scary Night

A library made a difference. Emily read her book of English fairy tales every minute she could find. She even sneaked the flashlight upstairs and read under the covers until Mama caught her at it. Fortunately there was a full moon and after Mama went downstairs again to read her own book, Emily was able to lean out the window and read by moonlight until she finished her chapter. The dove that turned into a handsome young man, the girl who had to bring water from the well in a sieve, the old woman whose pig would not go over the stile—Emily loved every word. Best of all she enjoyed scary stories, the tales of giants

and ogres and the one about the fair young woman with the golden arm who turned into a ghost. That was a spooky story. There had never been any scary, spooky stories in any of Emily's readers.

The book Mama was reading was a book of poetry and that made a difference, too, because now Mama went about her work reciting instead of singing. Mama would recite,

"*I remember, I remember*
The house where I was born,
The little window where the sun
Came peeping in at morn."

Emily could just picture Mama as a little girl waking up in the morning in a house back East. But Emily's favorite poem was a different one.

★ ★ ★

"Once upon a midnight dreary, while I
pondered weak and weary,
Over many a quaint and curious volume
of forgotten lore,"

Mama would say in a spooky voice as she fried the potatoes.

"While I nodded, nearly napping,
suddenly there came a tapping,
As of someone gently rapping, rapping at
my chamber door."

The way Mama said it gave Emily a shivery feeling between her shoulder blades. It was the scariest thing Emily had ever heard and she enjoyed every word of it, although she did not entirely understand it. The poem was about a raven that kept saying, or rather quothing, "Nevermore." "Quoth the Raven, 'Nevermore,'" was the way many of the stanzas ended.

"Say the spooky poem again, Mama," she would ask, and then shiver deliciously as Mama recited,

"Ah, distinctly I remember it was in the bleak December
And each separate dying ember wrought its ghost upon the floor."

Emily enjoyed spooky things when she knew she really had nothing to be scared about. Perhaps that was why Emily decided a spooky evening would be fun when her cousin June came to spend the night with her, or perhaps it was the still, expectant feeling of that hot, hot day that made her feel that something was about to happen. She decided that when bedtime came she and June could go upstairs to bed and tell spooky stories about witches and ghosts and have a good time scaring each other.

That is, they could if June would co-operate, but knowing June, Emily could not be sure of this. In school when Miss Plotkin led the singing she instructed the class to enunciate so that each word was distinct: "Ring out, ye bells." Emily and the rest of the class opened their mouths and moved their lips so that each word was separate from every other word. Ring—out—ye—bells. Not June. She sang loud and gleefully, "Ring *ow*chee bells." That was June for you. "Ring *ow*chee bells."

That evening after supper June, carrying her rolled-up nightgown and her toothbrush, was brought to Emily's house by Uncle Avery and Aunt Bessie, who were on their way to a whist party. "Hello, Emily," she said, when Emily opened the door, and Emily could tell from the way she said it that June was excited to be spending the night away from home. That was a good sign.

Then Emily discovered that this was the night Daddy had to go uptown for band practice. That made it even better. There was something scary about being alone in the great big house with Mama, something scary but cozy, too. Sometimes Emily enjoyed having Mama all to herself, although of course tonight June would be there, too.

Daddy practiced his solo, *Sailor, Beware*, on his baritone horn a couple of times before he went uptown to join the rest of the boys, as the men in the Pitchfork band were called. Everyone hoped that the band, which played at the State Fair and the Livestock Exposition, would help put Pitchfork on the map, although Emily knew that Pitchfork was already on the map. She had looked in the atlas at school and there it was, a tiny dot on the map of Oregon.

When Daddy had gone, Mama began to

read her library book while Emily and June studied the Montgomery Ward catalog to see what they would buy if they had any money. Emily looked, as she always did, at the picture of the rotary eggbeater, which could whip cream in no time at all. After that, she and June had difficulty looking at the catalog together, because Emily wanted to look at the beautiful toys some people must have enough money to buy and June wanted to look at all the different auto robes, many of them like real Indian blankets. Finally Emily let June take the catalog, because she was company. She herself looked at the book of wallpaper samples and pretended she could buy new wallpaper for the whole house. She would start with the downstairs bedroom, where a pattern of yellow roses would be pretty. Yellow was Mama's favorite color. She always said yellow was so gay.

Out on the back porch Plince whined

and scratched at the screen door.

Mama walked from the sitting room into the dining room and called, "What's the matter, Plince?"

Plince whimpered and tried to open the screen door with his paw.

Spooks, thought Emily. Plince must be scared of spooks.

"Now Plince, you run along and sleep in the woodshed the way you always do," Mama said, as she closed the door. Dogs were not allowed in the house any more than pigs or cows. They belonged outdoors.

"Plince sounded scared of something, didn't he?" Emily remarked when Mama sat down again.

"Now Emily," said Mama, "don't let your imagination run away with you." She said it with a smile, because Mama understood what many people did not—it was fun to let one's imagination run away. It made life exciting to let one's imagination go galloping off just the way a real horse had once made Mama's life pretty exciting for a while.

Emily decided it was time to produce the treat she had been saving—bananas! Grandpa had a whole bunch hanging in the window of his store, and when he heard that June was going to spend the night with Emily he had given Emily two bananas for a treat. When Emily went out to the kitchen to get them, Plince whined and scratched at the screen door once more.

The two girls peeled their bananas and began to eat. Emily ate with little bites, chewing as slowly as she could, to make the precious fruit last as long as she could. June bit off big pieces of the banana. "It tastes so much better in big bites," she explained.

"But it doesn't last as long," protested Emily.

"But it tastes better while it does last," said June.

"Now Emily," said Mama, "you can't

expect everyone to enjoy eating bananas the same way."

Of course she could not, but Emily wished she and June could do something the same way just once. If Muriel were here, she would understand immediately how a banana should be made to last as long as possible, even though in Portland she probably had bananas every day if she wanted them.

Plince persisted in scratching at the screen door. "Plince, stop that!" ordered Mama. The dog stopped scratching and began to whimper.

"Plince is a fraidy-cat," said June.

"You mean fraidy-dog," said Emily, and both girls giggled.

When the bananas were eaten, Emily turned to her mother. "Say the poem again. The spooky one."

Mama closed her book. "Just one verse," she said, and began, "'Once upon a midnight dreary—'" while outside a lilac bush began to scratch at the window as if it too wanted to come inside, and the curtains stirred in a ghostly way. When Mama finished the verse she said briskly, "Now off to bed you go."

"Just one more verse," begged Emily.

"Scoot," said Mama.

The girls washed their faces and brushed their teeth at the kitchen sink and tonight, because she had a guest, Emily picked up the flashlight to guide the way upstairs. Usually she went alone through the long dark hall and up the long dark flight of stairs to the dark bedroom and thought nothing of it. The house was dark, because each room had just one electric light hanging by a cord from the middle of the ceiling. The ceilings were high and all the Bartletts except Mama, who after all was not born a Bartlett, were tall people, so the lights were too high for Emily to reach without standing on a chair.

Mama could barely reach them by standing on tiptoe. The tall Bartletts had not wanted lights hanging where they could bump into them in the dark.

In the farthest bedroom the girls bounced into bed and pulled the quilts up under their chins, because now a cool breeze was blowing through the house. Emily played the flashlight around the big room. Its weak light made the white iron bedstead, the only furniture in the room, look ghostly. Even the windows, which had inside shutters instead of curtains, looked like oblong eyes in the night. "Isn't it scary?" whispered Emily. "And did you notice there was something funny about the way Plince wanted to come in the house?"

"Probably he just wanted a banana," scoffed June.

"Dogs don't eat bananas," said Emily, thinking that Muriel would have been a much more satisfactory cousin to be spending the night. Muriel would have enjoyed huddling in the middle of the bed making up ghost stories. June's imagination would never run away with her; she had an imagination like—like a plow horse.

The old house made a snapping noise. "I'll bet that was a ghost walking across the roof, wringing its hands," whispered Emily, trying to work up a good shiver in spite of June.

"It's the temperature changing," said June. "You know your house always makes noises when it begins to cool off."

This was the sort of thing Emily might have expected from matter-of-fact June, who was not entering into the spooky spirit of things. Emily tried again, still whispering because she had heard Mama come upstairs to bed. "Did you know this house has *thirteen* rooms?"

"Well," said June, "our great-grand-father had a big family. He needed a lot of rooms."

Oh, honestly, June, thought Emily crossly, you aren't being any fun at all. June was right, of course, but it would be fun to think for a little while that there was a ghost walking across the roof of a thirteen-room house, especially when Daddy was still uptown at band practice. It would be pleasantly scary if the pioneer ancestors had left a ghost or two around the house, perhaps in the cupola, but these ancestors must have been too busy clearing the land and settling the state of Oregon to participate in any ghostly activities like people in some of the sad old songs Mama sometimes sang. As far as Emily knew, there was not a brokenhearted damsel or a disappointed lover killed in a duel in the lot. They did get pretty hungry toward the end of their journey across the plains to Oregon, but nobody languished or wasted away. Apparently they ate a good square meal when they got to Oregon and went right to work cutting trees, pulling stumps, and planting crops. June was right. The house, even if it did have thirteen rooms, was not the least bit haunted.

Emily tried to think of something ghostly, but all she could think of was the skeleton of a cow down in the pasture and there was nothing ghostly about that. The cow did not die of a broken heart. It was a cow Daddy had to shoot because it ate some baling wire. It had been one of Daddy's best milkers and it was a shame that a cow that gave milk so rich in butterfat had to go eat baling wire.

And then Plince howled. It was a long-drawn-out, dismal, unearthly howl that began low in the scale and rose to a high, eerie note.

Each girl caught her breath. "June," whispered Emily, "do you know what that means?

When a dog howls it means somebody is going to *die!*"

This time June did not sound so matter-of-fact. "He's probably howling at the moon."

"There isn't any moon," said Emily, realizing for the first time that sometime during the evening the sky had clouded over. "It is a dark and cloudy night."

The girls huddled closer together in bed. Somewhere a loose shutter banged as persistently as if someone were trying to get in. Emily remembered a snatch of Mama's spooky poem about someone "rapping, rapping at my chamber door." Her heart pounded like the dasher of a churn.

Plince's howl rose and fell again in a way that made the girls shiver. The snap of the floor in the bedroom made them both start. They giggled nervously and lay still and tense. Plince's howl died and the night seemed unnaturally silent—as if it were waiting for something.

"His howl couldn't mean somebody is going to die," said June bravely. "Nobody in Pitchfork is even sick."

And then it came—a flash of lightning that for one instant made the bedroom seem as bright as midday and the white iron bedstead look like the bed of a ghost. The girls held their breath until the crash and roll of thunder seemed to shake the world.

"I—I guess Plince was howling because he knew there was going to be a storm," said Emily, relieved to have an explanation for the dog's peculiar behavior.

"Y-yes," agreed June. "I was almost scared there for a minute."

Once more lightning brought a flash of midday into the bedroom, and the girls waited for thunder to shatter the night. "One, two, three, four, five—" counted June, "—fifteen, sixteen." The thunder cracked. "The lightning struck sixteen miles away. If you count between the flash and the time you hear the thunder you can tell."

This was reassuring. Emily huddled against June, counting. Fifteen miles. Thirteen miles. The storm was moving slowly.

Then the rain began. The first big drops

hit the roof like a rattle of pebbles and then, as the thunder rolled on, the rain began to fall steadily with a drumming sound on the flat tin roof. The familiar sound of rain on the roof was comforting to Emily. She lay in bed thinking drowsily that she really liked June in spite of her plow-horse imagination. She was a sturdy girl and the best rope jumper and jacks player at school.

Emily may have fallen asleep—afterward she was not sure, because it seemed to her that she continued to hear thunder. Sometime later she became aware of a new sound in the night, a clanging banging sound that seemed very close, almost directly below on the back porch. This time her imagination was *not* running away with her. It couldn't be running away with her because she could not imagine what the noise was.

Emily sat up in bed. "June, what's that noise?" she asked aloud, to make herself heard above the wind and the rain.

June raised herself in bed and listened.

Wham. Bang. Crash. This was too strange. A dog's howl, thunder, rain—these were easily explained, but this. . . . Emily jumped out of bed and looked out of the window. Through the lashing branches of the horse chestnut tree she could see a ghostly white figure moving across the barnyard. She shut her eyes and opened them again. The ghostly figure really was there. She could see it with her own eyes.

"June!" Emily cried. "Look!"

June leaned on the sill beside her. This time she had no matter-of-fact explanation. "Oh!" She clutched Emily's arm. "It's a ghost and it's coming closer!"

"I'm going to get Mama." Emily snatched up the flashlight and ran across the cold floor to her mother's bedroom.

"Wait for me!" begged June.

For once the cousins felt the same way about something!

"Mama!" called Emily, beaming the flashlight on the bed. It was empty. There was no answer, only the rain drumming on the roof. *Wham. Bang. Crash.* Something seemed to be pounding on the back porch. Somewhere in the night Goliath the bull bellowed, and Emily wondered if the ghost was chasing him. "Mama's gone!"

"Maybe the ghost got her," said June with a shiver.

"Your imagination is running away with you," Emily told her cousin. But where could Mama be? Had the—the *thing* in the barnyard run off with her? Emily tried to say whoa to her imagination, but she could not. If only this had not been Daddy's band-practice night. . . .

"Maybe she's in the kitchen." June sounded shaky. "Let's go downstairs."

Clutching each other's hand, the girls made their way down the stairs. The thin beam of their flashlight seemed feeble in the darkness of the hall. A strong draft whipped at their nightgowns, telling them that the back door, which Mama had closed earlier in the evening, was now open. "Mama!" called Emily, and knew she was calling to an empty house.

The draft was even stronger in the dining room. The girls huddled shivering.

"The back door must have blown open," said June. "Maybe we should shut it. That— *thing* might—"

"Yes," agreed Emily quickly. "You shut it."

"It's your house," said June.

Neither girl wanted to shut the back door. "Let's both do it," said Emily, and fearfully they approached the door. When Emily turned the flashlight on it she revealed an enormous ragged hole torn in the screen.

"Look!" she cried, and in a panic slammed the door and leaned against it. "It—it must have been made by the ghost."

"Y-yes," agreed June.

"But a—a ghost wouldn't have to tear a hole in the screen," quavered Emily. "It would just float through."

"I hope it was leaving instead of coming in," said June. "Please, let's turn on a light someplace."

Wham. Bang. Crash.

"I'm too scared," said Emily, but she did swing the beam of the flashlight around the dining room and kitchen.

"Look!" cried June.

Emily looked, and there, cowering under the kitchen table, was Plince. She could have cried with relief. "It must have been Plince who tore the screen door. He was so scared he ran right through it."

"Yes, but what was he scared of?" June

wanted to know.

The dog flattened himself on the floor and crawled, whimpering, toward Emily, who stooped to pat him. Plince licked her hand gratefully and Emily felt almost as grateful to be touching a real live honest-to-goodness dog. But Mama—where was Mama? Could she have gone outdoors? On a night like this?

Bravely, ghost or no ghost, Emily returned to the back door and, as she opened it, Goliath bellowed again somewhere out there in the night. It was terrible when something as big and as mean-looking as Goliath was scared. Emily turned her flashlight into the night. The wind and the rain seemed to snatch the feeble beam and twist it into a nightmare shape against the lashing horse chestnut tree, but Emily caught a glimpse of a ghostly figure—a figure with a pitchfork in its hand. "June!" she screamed, dropping the flashlight. "It *is* a ghost! A ghost with a pitchfork!" Maybe they had a ghostly pioneer ancestor after all.

June clung to Emily. "Is it coming to get us?" she asked, terrified.

Wham. Bang. Crash.

The ghost yelled, "You get out of here!" The ghost's voice—no, Daddy's voice—tossed and twisted by the wind, reached the terrified girls. Emily felt weak with relief. Whatever it was, it was going to be all right. Daddy was home from band practice. And if Daddy was home, Mama, wherever she was, was safe. They were all safe.

Wham. Bang. Crash.

Once more lightning, like a terrible swift sword, split the sky and illuminated the whole scene. The ghost was Daddy! Daddy in his white nightshirt! Pitchfork in hand, he was facing Goliath the bull, who had Mama's copper wash boiler caught on his horns.

Wham. Bang. Crash. Emily understood the sound now. It was Goliath banging the wash boiler against the fence trying to get it off his horns. There was no longer anything frightening about the sound. "It's just Goliath," she said. "He must have got out somehow."

Cold as they were, the girls huddled in the doorway, hoping for another bolt of lightning to show them what was going on. They could tell that Daddy was getting the bull back to the barn, because the racket gradually moved off through the barnyard.

The girls returned to the kitchen, where they stood rubbing their arms to get warm. Soon Emily climbed on a kitchen chair to turn on the light. How different the world seemed by the light of one bulb! Ghostly shapes became tables and chair. Plince dozed with his nose on his paws, just as if he was allowed in the house. To Emily's surprise the hands on the alarm clock on the shelf pointed to one o'clock.

One o'clock in the *morning!* Never had she been up so late, not even when she got to go with Mama and Daddy to the doings at the Masonic Hall last winter. "Just think, June," she said. "We have been up all night, because it is morning now."

"I think it still counts as night until about five o'clock." By the light of electricity June had become her old sturdy self again. "Besides we must have gone to sleep."

"I'm sure I didn't sleep a wink," said Emily, who wanted to believe she had been up all night. "I was listening for ghosts."

"There's no such thing as ghosts." Now June could say this. Things were different a little while ago.

Now Mama came running up on the back porch but not with her high heels tapping. She was wearing rubbers over her bare feet and an old coat over her nightgown. Her shiny black hair hung over her shoulder in a braid.

"Mama, where were you?" asked Emily.

"In the door of the woodshed with a pitch-fork, in case your father needed me," she answered, as she stuffed paper and kindling into the stove to start a fire. "He finally got Goliath tied up in the barn and is trying to get the wash boiler off his horns. My good copper wash boiler." She touched a match to the paper, and the fire began to crackle cheerfully.

So Mama had been standing by ready to attack Goliath with a pitchfork if she was needed. How silly to have thought a mere ghost could run off with Mama. Mama would not have stood for it. She had too much spunk.

"Nothing exciting like this ever happens at home." June sounded wistful. "All we ever have in the night is a cat fight once in a while."

"Girls, you must go to bed," insisted Mama. "Scoot. This very minute."

For the second time that night the two cousins ran upstairs and snuggled into bed. Emily felt warm and cozy now that she knew Daddy was home.

"I love to spend the night here," said June drowsily.

"M–hm." Emily was too sleepy to answer. She had had her scary night after all—a little too scary maybe—but it was nice to know that in a pinch June had a runaway imagination too. Emily wriggled closer to her cousin and fell fast asleep.

7

Emily and The Light Flaky Pie Crust

Emily loved to watch Grandma measure out dress material on the dry-goods side of the store. Times were hard that year and the ladies who bought dress goods did not want to buy one inch more than they needed. Grandma would take the dress pattern and lay it out on the material before she cut the goods from the bolt. All the ladies in the store would gather around and watch, while Grandma figured and figured how to save material.

Emily leaned against the counter and watched. She listened, too, and she learned all sorts of interesting things. She learned, for example, that Arlene Twitchell never ate the crusts of her sandwiches. That was bad enough, but the shameful part was that her mother did not expect her to eat the crusts. She trimmed the crusts off Arlene's sandwiches herself. The way she spoiled that girl! And the way the boys admired Arlene! Well . . .

Emily did not see why anyone should expect Arlene to eat the crusts of her sandwiches. Arlene not only had curly hair, she was the prettiest girl in town. Who was Liberty holding aloft a cardboard torch in the Fourth of July parade? Arlene, of course. Who was crowned Queen of the May in front of the high school? Arlene, who else? It was girls like Emily who had to eat the crusts of sandwiches as well as carrots and burnt toast, in the hope that their hair might curl.

Emily learned lots of other things while Grandma laid out patterns on goods. She learned that Grandma Russell, a lady so old the whole town called her Grandma, had climbed up on her roof and mended the shingles herself, and she was eighty-two if she was a day. It just showed what a little pioneer blood in the veins could do for a person. Once Emily ducked under the counter, because Fong Quock came into the store, and while she sat there among the paper bags, she heard one of the ladies telling someone that the secret of the lightest, flakiest pie crust you ever saw was adding a generous pinch of baking powder to the dough.

Emily pricked up her ears at this bit of information. A generous pinch of baking powder added to the dough made a light, flaky pie crust. She must remember to tell Mama. When Mama baked a pie she always apologized. "I don't know what the trouble is, but my pie crust isn't as light as it should be."

Daddy always answered, "It tastes good to me." Emily did not like pie crust, so she usually ate the filling and left the crust. No one ever said eating pie crust made hair curly.

Emily forgot about the cooking secret she had in her possession until one Sunday morning at breakfast, when Mama suddenly exclaimed, "My land! This is the day of the potluck dinner at the church. I've been so busy it completely slipped my mind."

"What are we going to take?" asked Emily.

Mama dropped into a chair to think a minute. She was dog-tired from all the work that summer. Finally she said, "Emily, I'm afraid we can't stay for the dinner after the church service. There isn't time to kill and fry some chickens and there isn't a thing in the house I can take."

Miss the potluck dinner at the church! Emily was dreadfully disappointed. That meant she would have to go to Sunday school and then come home, while all the other boys and girls stayed for church and the dinner. "Isn't there anything we can take?" she pleaded. "Remember, Mama, you said you would remind the minister to say something about more donations for the library."

Daddy, who had eaten a big bowl of oatmeal with thick cream and a plate of bacon, eggs, and fried potatoes, said, "We always have plenty of milk and eggs. What about custard pies?"

"I don't have time to make pies before church," answered Mama.

Emily could not bear missing that potluck dinner, especially when the library might be announced from the pulpit. "Mama, could I make custard pies?" she asked. "If I skipped Sunday school and went to church instead, there would be time. Please, Mama."

Mama smiled at Emily. "Perhaps you could. At least you could help me. Come on, let's go to work."

While Mama cleared the kitchen table, Emily got out the breadboard, the rolling pin, and the pie pans. Daddy put another stick of wood in the stove so the fire would not die down. Emily took a big bowl from the pantry shelf. "Tell me what to put in," she called to Mama in the kitchen.

"Two and a half cups of flour," directed Mama. "Some salt—not quite a teaspoonful. Let's see, some lard. You'd better let me measure that." Mama came into the pantry and deftly measured the lard out of the lard bucket. "Now Emily, take two knives and slash through the flour and lard until it is as fine as corn meal."

Emily started to slash. She was about to mention her secret for a light, flaky pie crust, but then she decided no, she would surprise Mama. She would surprise the whole congregation with her pie crust. People who chose her pie for dessert would take one bite and say, "What light, flaky pie crust! I wonder who baked it." Then Emily would smile modestly and Mama would say, "Emily baked it." And all the ladies would ask her for the secret of her light, flaky crust. Quickly Emily added a generous pinch of baking powder and then, not certain how big a generous pinch should be, added another generous pinch to make sure. Then she slashed and slashed and according to Mama's directions, added water, just a little bit.

"There are two secrets to making good

pie crust," said Mama. "Use very little water and handle the dough lightly."

Emily smiled to herself because she knew a third secret. She dumped out the dough on the breadboard. It looked more like a pile of crumbs than pie crust. When she rolled she got flat crumbs instead of pie crust. She rolled a little harder.

"Lightly, Emily," said Mama. "Lightly."

It was no use. The crumbs would not become crust. Mama came and took the rolling pin from Emily. She scooped the crumbs into a pile, gave them a gentle squeeze and a pat, and rolled them out. Pie crust!

"Now let me," pleaded Emily. This part was fun. She draped the crust over the pie tins and slash, slash, trimmed off the ragged edges. Then she tucked under the edges and pressed her thumb around the edge to make neat scallops, just the way Mama did.

Preparing the filling was much easier and soon Emily had her pie shells filled with liquid custard the color of buttercups. Mama tested the oven by holding her hand inside a moment before she set the pies to bake.

While Emily and Mama dressed for church, the kitchen was filled with the sweet fragrance of custard. Emily could just see her pies among the others on one of the tables in the church basement. Golden yellow and freckled with nutmeg . . .

"Emily, I think it is time to test the pies," said Mama. "Insert a knife and if it comes out clean, they are done."

How good the pies smelled! Emily was filled with anticipation as she found a clean knife. Carefully she opened the oven door and peeked inside. She could not believe what she saw. Her beautiful buttercup-colored pies! Whatever could have happened to them? "Mama!" shrieked Emily. "Come here quick!"

Mama's high heels came tapping down the stairs. "What is it, Emily?"

"My pies!" wailed Emily. "Look!"

Mama leaned over and looked into the oven. "My land, Emily," she exclaimed, "the crust is on top!"

"I put it on the bottom," said Emily. "How did it get on top?"

"I don't know but I'm sure the pies must be done." Using pot holders, Mama lifted the pies out and set them on the table to cool. They were strange-looking pies. They had nicely browned crusts with little patches of custard showing through here and there.

"We can't take them to church." Emily was wilted with disappointment. "Now we'll have to miss the potluck dinner and the minister will forget to announce about the library."

Daddy came into the kitchen to examine the cooling pies. "I don't see why we can't take them to church," he said. "There is no reason why a pie can't taste just as good with the crust on top as on the bottom."

"I just don't understand it," said Mama. "It must be something about my oven."

"It was my fault," confessed Emily reluctantly and told how she had planned to surprise the congregation with light, flaky pie crust by adding a generous pinch of baking powder. She was surprised when both Mama and Daddy thought her story was funny.

"That crust is light all right," said Daddy. "It is so light it floated right up through the custard."

Mama examined the pies more closely. "You know, the crust really does look light and flaky. All it needed was to be weighed down by a filling of apples or raisins. Now don't worry, Emily. We'll wrap up the pies and take them along to church. I'll unwrap them when no one is looking and there will be so many pies no one will even notice."

"I'll eat two pieces," said Daddy loyally.

And so the Bartletts set off for church with the two pies carefully wrapped in clean dish towels. Emily was wearing her Sunday-school hat, which she did not like one bit. Grandma, who could trim such beautiful hats for ladies, had very definite ideas about what was proper for girls Emily's age. Emily longed for a hat trimmed with garlands of flowers, clouds of veiling, and maybe an ostrich plume or two, and what did she get? A stiff black Milan hat with a wide brim, a black ribbon hanging down the back, and an elastic under the chin to keep it on. Mama said Emily had the most beautiful hat of any girl in Pitchfork, but Emily had a different opinion of it. It was such a problem, loving Grandma and not liking her little-girl hats.

Sunday school was over when the Bartletts arrived at the little white church, and all the boys and girls were out in the churchyard, playing tag to stretch their legs before the service began. Emily's cousin June came running over. "Are you bringing pie?" she asked, and Emily noticed that, as usual, one of her barrettes was slipping.

"Yes, June," answered Mama. "Emily did a little baking."

"What kind?" demanded June.

Mama hesitated a second. "Custard," she replied. There would probably be a dozen custard pies at the dinner.

"We brought coleslaw," said June, and bounded off to try to chin herself on a branch of a locust tree whose leaves were turning yellow.

"Why, there's Fong Quock," observed Mama, while Emily looked quickly off in another direction. Then she felt guilty.

Fong Quock had given a whole dollar to the library.

"I hope he is bringing rice," said Daddy. When Fong Quock was younger and Pitchfork was smaller, he had given a party for the whole town once a year. He served Chinese food and Daddy had never forgotten Fong Quock's rice.

Emily and Mama carried the pies down the steps to the church basement, where some ladies were bustling about setting tables, which were boards laid over sawhorses, and measuring coffee into salt sacks to dangle inside the big graniteware coffeepots. Mama nodded and smiled pleasantly at everyone, and when no one was looking she slipped the dish towels off the pies and set them on a table with the rest of the desserts.

"Mama, I don't see any other custard pies," whispered Emily.

"Don't worry. There will be," Mama assured her.

Emily was not so sure. Maybe none of the ladies of Pitchfork felt like baking custard pie today. Maybe hers would be the only ones. And June would be sure to blurt out that Emily had baked them. June was a great one for blurting things out.

The church bells began to ring and Emily thought distinctly Ring—out—ye—bells, as she had been taught at school, and filed into the church with Mama and Daddy. Emily felt proud to be sitting in the pew beside Daddy. He looked so big and handsome in his dark suit.

Emily always suffered a terrible temptation in church, because the brown paint on the backs of the pews was blistered and she longed to puncture the blisters to see the gray paint underneath. She glanced down the pew and there was her cousin June busily puncturing the paint blisters. Yield not to temptation, Emily told herself sternly, and tried not to squirm or think about her custard pies.

Emily forgot about her pies when Mr. Bonnett, the minister, stood up and actually did announce the library from the pulpit. He gave a little talk about the good ladies who were giving so generously of their time to bring books to the people of Pitchfork, and how they would welcome donations of money and good books, and what a fine thing a library would be for the boys and girls growing up in Pitchfork.

And the boy who walks down the railroad track with his clean white flour sack, Emily added to herself.

Then Mr. Bonnett began his text for the day—the miracle of the loaves and fishes. Emily enjoyed the story of Jesus feeding the multitudes with five loaves of bread and two fishes, but as Mr. Bonnett went on and on, Emily found it difficult to sit still and she was sure the elastic on her hat would choke her before the sermon ended. Mr. Bonnett reminded the congregation that the people of Pitchfork should have faith. It was faith that had fed the multitudes.

Emily felt squirmier and squirmier. In Pitchfork, where everything grew so readily, it was easy to have enough faith to feed the multitudes. It was harder to have faith about things like libraries, but if faith would help, Emily would have faith. She squirmed some more and caught Mama frowning at her. To keep herself still, she sat at attention the way she had learned at school—eyes ahead, back straight, feet on the floor, hands folded—and had faith that Pitchfork would get a real library. The trouble was, the elastic on her hat was so tight. If only Grandma would let her have the kind of grown-up hat that was held on with hatpins instead of this elastic under the chin. . . .

What a relief it was to be able to stand up and sing the final hymn:

"Bringing in the sheaves, bringing in the sheaves,
We shall come rejoicing, bringing in the sheaves."

This was Emily's favorite hymn. When she sang it she could just see Daddy at harvesttime striding along with sheaves of wheat in his arms.

As soon as she could, Emily scampered down the steps and around to the door of the church basement. By the time she got there she had her hat off. She hung it on a hook and sidled over to the table of desserts.

If there was one thing the ladies of Pitchfork were good at, it was baking. There were cakes, all kinds of cakes— pound cake, Lady Baltimore cake, angel cake, devil's food (was it really all right to bring devil's food to church, Emily wondered), pineapple upside-down cake with a cherry in each circle of pineapple, walnut loaf cake, the kind without frosting. And there were pies, too. Cherry pie with the top crust made of woven strips. Apple pie. Emily could see the cinnamon through the slashes in the crusts. Lemon pie with meringue in delicate peaks. Blackberry pies with crimson juice oozing through the crust. And custard pies, two of them— Emily's.

The only thing Emily could do was pretend she knew nothing about the pies and hope that June would forget them. She found a place at a bench beside Daddy at one of the long tables. Mama was busy helping some of the other ladies serve the food.

June came along and plopped herself down on the bench beside Emily. "I'm hungry," June announced. "I could eat a horse."

Emily felt suddenly shy when Mr. Bonnett sat down opposite her. He was such an important man, a man who could stand up in the pulpit and speak to the multitudes about the library. Whatever could she find to say to him, this man who could speak to the multitudes?

The food the ladies set on the table! Platters of fried chicken. Bowls of chicken and dumplings. String beans that had simmered for hours with bits of bacon. Huge pans of escaloped potatoes. Bowls of coleslaw, the cabbage sliced thin as paper. And rice. Fong Quock had brought a huge kettle of rice. His rice was the despair of all the ladies in Pitchfork. All their husbands asked for rice the way Fong Quock cooked it, but no matter how hard they tried, none of the ladies could cook rice so that each grain was separate and fluffy and there was crisp brown crust on the bottom of the kettle. The ladies of Pitchfork burned a lot of rice trying.

Now Emily had another problem to take her mind off her custard pies and what to say to the minister. That was chicken. At every single Christmas or Thanksgiving dinner, family reunion, church dinner, or lodge supper someone always served Emily, and said, as if offering a great treat, "And here is a drumstick for Emily." Emily did not like drumsticks. She longed for white meat, the piece with the wishbone in it, but always it was drumsticks, drumsticks, drumsticks.

Today, however, turned out to be

different. A platter of chicken was passed to June, who helped herself to two drumsticks before she passed the heavy platter to Emily, who had to rest it on the table.

"May I help you, Emily?" asked Mr. Bonnett.

"No, thank you, I can manage," said Emily hastily, because there were still drumsticks left. She helped herself to the wishbone piece, with a feeling of triumph. She would take it home to dry in the warming oven and when it was brittle she would use it to make a wish. She would wish for *Black Beauty*, because that was a little, selfish wish. Faith was for big, unselfish things like a library for the whole town.

After that things were better. Mr. Bonnett did most of the talking, so Emily did not have to worry about what to say to him. He talked about the splendid work the Ladies' Aid was doing for the church. He talked about the need for more partitions in the Sunday-school room. He praised the cooking of the ladies of Pitchfork. When Emily finished her chicken, she wiped the wishbone on her napkin and slipped it inside her bloomer leg. Emily found bloomer legs handy for carrying all sorts of things—rubber balls, jacks, even a jumping rope.

With Mr. Bonnett talking so much and everyone having to stop eating to listen politely, naturally Emily's table was the last to finish. Emily looked out of the corner of her eye at the table of desserts. There was nothing left but two pies, Emily's custard pies. Naturally they were left to the last—they were such peculiar-looking pies. One of the ladies was cutting them now. How perfectly dreadful! Emily wanted to crawl under the table she was so embarrassed.

Of course one of the ladies served the

minister first. "I'm not quite sure what kind of pie this is," she said apologetically. "It looks like custard, but the crust is on top."

"Is that the pie you baked?" June asked Emily.

Emily nodded.

"Well, well," said Mr. Bonnett, in a voice that reached the multitudes in the church basement. "So this little lady baked the pie!"

Emily squirmed on the hard bench. Everyone turned to look at the little lady who baked the pies. The minister looked around at the people at his table. Then he looked at the pies. "Wait a minute," he said. "There are twelve pieces of pie and twenty people at the table. There isn't enough to go around." He picked up a knife and cut each piece of pie into two pieces. "There now, that is more like it," he said. "Enough to go around and second helpings for some.

Like the loaves and fishes, eh, Emily?" He
laughed heartily at his own joke.

Feeding the multitudes her custard pie
was the last thing Emily wanted to do. Since

she had baked it, she felt duty-bound to take a piece, too, even though she did not care much for anything as slippery-feeling as custard pie. What would people think if she was not willing to eat her own pie?

"It's awfully funny custard pie," remarked June.

Then Emily had an inspiration. "It is called upside-down pie," she said. Upside-down cake—why not upside-down pie? Let people think the crust was supposed to be on top.

The minister ate a mouthful of pie. "Delicious," he pronounced it. "The crust is light and flaky."

Everyone at the table murmured in agreement. Emily's pie crust *was* light and flaky. They said exactly what Emily had planned they should say, before her crust had risen through the custard.

"You know," remarked one of the ladies

thoughtfully, "having the crust on top is an excellent idea for custard pie. So often the crust on the bottom becomes soggy. Tell me, Emily, what is the secret of such a light, flaky crust?"

Emily smiled modestly. "I add a generous pinch of baking powder," she said.

8
The Hard-Times Party

Mama was heartsick, just heartsick, when Daddy told her how little money he would get for his crops that year. The barn was full, the sheep grew long thick wool, the hogs were fat, and what happened? The price of everything went way down and all Daddy's hard work earned scarcely enough money to see the Bartletts through the next year. To Emily this meant half-soled shoes, dresses that would have to be let down a second time, practical Christmas presents. That would be the worst part—practical Christmas presents.

"Mama, what will we do?" Emily asked anxiously.

"We'll manage somehow," Mama answered with a sad smile. "We always do. Just remember your pioneer ancestors. Their first winter in Oregon was so hard some of them had to make clothes out of the tops of their covered wagons."

Emily felt better. Twice-let-down dresses were better than clothes made out of covered-wagon tops, which must have been stiff and scratchy.

Times were hard for Grandpa, too. Farmers, who had charged their shoes and overalls and sugar and spices, often could not pay all their bills when their crops were sold. Yes, everybody in Pitchfork had to scrimp and pinch, and Emily knew there would be little money to give to the library that winter. What she did not expect, however, was that in a year when people had no money for the picture show or for gasoline to go riding around in their automobiles, they came to the library. During that hard winter there often were not enough books to go around. The state library sent three crates at a time instead of one, but still no *Black Beauty.* Mama checked books in and checked them right out again. One raw rainy afternoon Emily was so afraid there would not be any books left for the boy with the white flour sack that she selected a book for him and one for his little sister and hid them until he arrived, cold and wet from his long walk down the railroad track.

And what did the ladies of Pitchfork do about the library? They decided to have a party, a hard-times party, in the Masonic

Hall. They would charge twenty-five cents admission, proceeds to go to the library.

"Aren't hard times a funny thing to have a party about?" Emily asked. Parties were for birthdays and Valentines and Halloween. Happy occasions.

Mama smiled. "Perhaps it is, but I think it is a nice idea. It is better to have some fun out of life as we go along than to feel sorry for ourselves."

Emily wanted to have some fun out of life as she went along, too, and she wanted a chance to wear her best winter dress, the red taffeta with the gathered skirt that Grandma made for her last year. "Mama, could I go to the party this once?" she asked.

Usually when Mama and Daddy went out in the evening, Emily spent the night with Grandma and Grandpa in their rooms upstairs over the store. She loved Saturday night in Grandpa's store, because that was the night the loggers came to town.

The store was crowded with big noisy men in Mackinaws. The counters were piled high with groceries that night. Beans and coffee and great slabs of bacon and cheese—cartons and cartons of food were carried off to the logging camps on Saturday night. And when Emily's bedtime came, Grandma sent her upstairs, where she did not have to go straight to bed the way she did at home. She sat in Grandpa's Morris chair and read the dictionary with its limp leather cover and its colored illustrations of different breeds of cattle and all the flags in the world.

Emily was willing to miss Saturday night at the store if she could go to the hard-times party and Mama finally said she could, just this once. Emily listened with great interest when the ladies who came to the library talked about the party. They agreed to gather up all the red-and-white checked tablecloths in town for the tables, and they would serve baked beans, brown bread, and coleslaw.

Just for fun they would serve coffee from tin cans. This seemed appropriate to hard times and the ladies on the clean-up committee would not have to wash coffeepots. They could throw the cans away.

It all sounded like fun to Emily until Mama began to wonder what to wear.

"Your gray silk," said Emily. What else would Mama wear to a party but her best dress?

"But this is a hard-times party," said Mama. "We are supposed to wear hard-times costumes. I thought you knew that."

Emily had not known. "What are hard-times costumes?"

"Our oldest and most ragged clothes," Mama explained. "Any old thing we can find."

Emily was aghast. "What for?" she demanded.

"For fun," said Mama.

Fun! This was not Emily's idea of fun. Her idea of fun was dressing up in her best dress so that the ladies of Pitchfork would say, "Look at Emily Bartlett. Doesn't she look nice in her party dress?"

No, Emily made up her mind that she was not going to wear any old ragged dress to the party. Never. And so one evening when Mama got out Daddy's oldest overalls and began to sew patches on them, Emily was most disapproving. Mama did not sew on blue denim patches cut from another pair of old overalls. She sewed on pink and yellow and green flowery patches from the gayest scraps in the scrap bag, and she did not even sew them over holes. She sewed them any old place.

Suddenly Mama put down her sewing and burst out laughing. "Emily, I've had the most wonderful idea! I'm going to wash some gunny sacks and cut armholes and a neckhole in one for a blouse and make a skirt out of two more. And I'll make a belt out of—let's see—your father's socks pinned together with safety pins. And for a necklace—what shall I use for a necklace?"

Emily was too horrified to answer. Mama going to a party in gunny sacks! What a perfectly terrible idea.

"I know!" Mama was delighted with her inspiration. "I'll save squash seeds and string them for a necklace. And I'll braid my hair in two pigtails and tie them with bows of the twine your father uses for sewing gunny sacks."

This was getting worse and worse. Mama's beautiful black hair tied with gunny-sack twine! This time it was Mama's imagination that was running away with her.

"And Emily," Mama went on, not even noticing Emily's disapproval, "do you know what I think would be terribly funny?"

Emily was afraid to guess what Mama might think was terribly funny.

"I think it would be funny if you dressed up in a gunny sack, too." Mama was delighted with her idea. "I have a feeling we would be the belles of the ball."

A terrible feeling of rebellion rose up within Emily. She did not want to be funny. She did not want Mama to be funny. It was not dignified and grown-ups should always be dignified. And as for being the belles of the ball—to Emily being the belle of the ball meant the time she had heard Mama tell about. It was when she first came out West to teach school and before she met Daddy. Mama had gone to a dance with the people she boarded with in the little town where she was teaching. She was a new girl in town and what a whirl she had! All the young men wanted to dance with Mama, but there was one, tall and handsome and a real gentleman, who danced with her most of all. Mama had a wonderful time that evening, but a few days later it turned out that the tall, handsome gentleman was a horse thief who had to go to jail. Mama was very sorry to learn this, but she certainly had a story to write to her city cousins back East who had never danced with horse thieves. All this never would have happened if Mama had worn a gunny sack.

"We'll find some gunny sacks tomorrow," Mama went on, as if Emily had agreed, "and you can wear one of my old stockings for a belt."

"I won't," said Emily flatly.

"Won't what?" asked Mama, surprised.

"Won't wear any old gunny sack to the party," said Emily, "and I won't wear any old stocking for a belt either."

"But Emily—" Mama began.

"Well, I won't," said Emily. "I just won't."

"But Emily," protested Mama, "it would be so funny if we both appeared wearing gunny sacks."

Emily did not want to cross Mama, but she would *not* wear a gunny sack to the party.

Mama was not the only one in the family who had spunk.

"Emily," said Mama, "if a bee came along right now it would sting your lip."

No bee was going to come along in the Bartlett sitting room on a winter evening, but Emily pulled in her lip anyway.

"But why, Emily?" asked Mama.

It was impossible to explain to Mama about what it meant to be the belle of the ball, and that parties were for dressing up and looking beautiful. "Because," answered Emily, and had to remember not to let her lip stick out.

Then Daddy spoke from the table where he had been going over the bills. "Emily, you will wear what your mother tells you to wear or you will spend the night with your grandparents." When Daddy said something he meant it.

Mama looked thoughtfully at Emily. "If

she is going to the party she should have a good time. What do you want to wear, Emily?"

"My red party dress," said Emily promptly.

"All right," agreed Mama. "You bring it here and I'll baste some patches on it."

Mama still did not understand. "But Mama," said Emily, "I don't want patches on it. I want to wear it just the way it is. I want to dress up to go to the party." She wanted to be admired, not laughed at.

"All right," said Mama with a sigh. "Have it your way."

Then Emily felt terrible. She wished she could please Mama by wanting to wear a gunny sack to the party, but she could not.

The day of the party Emily helped Mama by tying bits of green thread around the handles of the silverware they were going to take, so they could tell their knives and forks and spoons from those of everyone else. Nothing was said about costumes until after supper, when Mama took down her long black hair and braided it into two pigtails which she tied with twine.

"Oh, Emily," said Mama with a laugh. "Don't look so disapproving. Run along and put on your party dress."

So Emily took her best winter party dress out of the wardrobe in the downstairs bedroom and put it on. It was a little tighter across the chest than she remembered, but she turned and twirled in front of the mirror in Mama's bird's-eye maple dresser and was pleased with herself as far down as she could see. Then she took her Mary Janes out of the wardrobe, but when she squeezed her feet into them they turned out to be so short she could not even wiggle her toes. Emily did not know what to do. People had been telling her she was growing like a weed and it was pleasant to know she was this much closer to being grown-up, but it was most uncomfortable to have it happen on this particular night.

Then Mama, wearing her gunny sacks, came gaily into the bedroom where she, too, turned and twirled in front of the mirror, just as if she were dressed in the latest fashion right out of a Butterick pattern book. Daddy, looking like a walking ragbag, came in and grinned at himself in the mirror. He put his hands on Mama's waist and lifted her off the floor. "You don't weigh enough to fill up even one gunny sack," he told her.

"Do I look nice?" Emily asked.

Mama and Daddy exchanged a quick glance that Emily did not understand. "Very nice," answered Mama.

Emily did not like to mention her shoes, especially when times were so hard and there was no money for more Mary

Janes, but they were pinching unbearably. "Mama . . . I think my shoes are too small."

Mama knelt and felt Emily's toes. "Why, they are way too short," she agreed. "Your toes are pushing right against the end. I'm afraid you will have to wear your everyday shoes."

"Oh Mama . . ." Emily felt she could not wear scuffed brown Oxfords with a party dress, but there was nothing else to do. She had no other shoes.

"Emily," said Mama suddenly, "how would you like to wear a pair of my old shoes? You could wear your Oxfords until we got there and then change."

Would Emily like to wear a pair of high-heeled shoes to the party? *Would* she? Of course the shoes would not fit, even though Mama's feet were small and Emily's were rather large, but even so, she would be the envy of all the girls there. "Oh, Mama, could I really?" Emily asked eagerly. Sometimes Mama let her try on the high-heeled shoes, but to get to wear them, actually *wear* them . . . It would help make up for Mama's going out in public in a gunny-sack dress.

And so the Bartletts set out for the Masonic Hall with an extra pair of Mama's old shoes in one paper bag and their silverware marked with green thread in another. As soon as they arrived Emily took off her own shoes and slipped into Mama's.

To Emily's relief, Mama hurried upstairs to help the ladies set the tables, without taking off her coat. Emily sat down on a folding chair at the side of the hall to look around her. Other boys and girls were running and sliding on the dance floor or jumping off the stage, but Emily, in Mama's high-heeled shoes, felt too grown-up for such childishness. June was there, running and sliding with the others. She was wearing an old middy, the skirt she tore one time when she tried to climb a barbed-wire fence, and a pair of mismated shoes, one a high brown shoe that laced and the other a Mary Jane so old the patent leather was cracked. She looked ragged and untidy, but, knowing June, Emily decided she probably did not care.

Emily looked around at the other costumes. The things that had been pulled out of trunks and ragbags! Moths certainly had been busy in Pitchfork. Old-fashioned trousers, hobble skirts that had gone out of style, patched and faded overalls and house dresses, skirts made out of flour sacks. One lady wore a man's straw hat trimmed with weeds. Another had used bread flour to powder her nose. Everyone gasped when the barber arrived with his head bandaged and his arm in a sling, but it turned out the bandages were part of his costume. Then Mr. Archer, the banker, arrived with a tomato-soup can tied on top of his head like Happy Hooligan in the funny papers, and Emily could not help laughing, he looked so funny.

Nobody in the whole crowd looked nice except Arlene Twitchell, the prettiest girl in town, who had a few pink patches basted to her best dress. She did look pretty, but in contrast to all the funny costumes, she also looked just plain stuck-up.

And then Emily knew she herself had done the wrong thing. She was going to look stuck-up, too. Mama had been right. Sometimes it was fun to make people laugh. Emily pulled her feet as far back under the chair as she could and buttoned her coat up under her chin. She did not want people to think that she was too stuck-up to wear a hard-times costume.

Bertie Young, the barber's son, skated across the floor. "Hello, Emily. Want to smell my haircut?"

Emily inhaled deeply as he leaned over. M-m-m. Carnation this time.

June came skidding across the floor. "Hello, Emily," she said, stopping in front of her cousin. "How come you don't take your coat off?"

"I don't feel like it," answered Emily truthfully.

"Come on," coaxed June. "Let's see your costume."

Emily did not quite know what to answer, but she knew that if she did not say something June would persist. "I . . . I didn't wear a costume," she admitted unhappily.

"Why not?" asked June.

"Because," answered Emily.

This was not enough for June. "Because why?"

"Because I didn't feel like it." Emily wished June would go back to sliding and leave her alone.

"I'll bet you are too stuck-up," accused June.

"I am not!"

"Then take off your coat and come sliding with the rest of us," said June.

"I can't," said Emily, searching for an answer. "I—I'm wearing high heels."

"High heels!" squeaked June, quite plainly impressed. "Golly." She bent over and peered under the chair at Emily's feet. "And you aren't spoofing, either. Hey, kids! Come here! Emily's wearing high heels."

Emily found herself surrounded by an interested crowd of ragamuffins who made her feel more dressed-up and uncomfortable than ever. The boys scoffed at her for wearing silly old high heels, but the girls were impressed. Their mothers would never let them wear high heels. Not until they were as old as Arlene Twitchell, who was so old she was as good as grown-up. Some of the girls, Emily could see, were thinking, That stuck-up Emily Bartlett!

More and more people arrived—hoboes and Charlie Chaplins and ladies gowned in whatever their ragbags had to offer. Almost everyone in Pitchfork had come to the party, which meant a lot of twenty-five-cent pieces for the library. Mama came downstairs in her gunny-sack dress, which everyone admired and laughed at. Emily felt worse and worse.

Then Mrs. Warty Thompson sat down at the piano on the stage and pounded out some good loud chords to attract the attention of the crowd. The boys and girls stopped sliding and everyone was quiet.

"Hear ye, hear ye, hear ye!" shouted Uncle Avery, the mayor, who was wearing an old baseball uniform.

"You tell 'em!" yelled the barber.

"Get ready for the grand march," directed Uncle Avery. "Around the hall until the judges decide which couples are the best-dressed of this crowd of fashionably dressed citizens!"

"Hooray!" shouted the barber. "Let's go!"

Mrs. Warty Thompson struck up a march, the same one she always played for the crowning of the Queen of the May. *Dum* dum de dum . . .

Two by two the crowd began to form a procession.

"Come on, Emily," said June. "You can march with me."

Emily drew back. "I think I would rather watch."

"Now Emily." Mama spoke firmly. "You

wanted to come to the party. Now be a good sport."

"But Mama," said Emily in a desperate whisper, "I'm too dressed up. Everybody will think I am stuck-up."

Mama looked as if she were amused at something. "I wouldn't worry about that if I were you," she said. "Take off your coat and go along with June."

Emily could see that Mama expected to be obeyed. There was nothing to do but shed her coat and join the marchers. Let people see her in her best dress and high heels—there was nothing she could do about it now. She took only one step before she slipped on the polished floor. She had to clutch June to regain her balance.

Emily curled her toes under, as hard as she could, to make the shoes fit better. Walking was not easy, but she stumped along on her curled-up toes the best she could, clinging to June's arm for support. Her ankles bowed out and when she tried to straighten them, they caved in. It was a good thing June was such a sturdy cousin.

Around the Masonic Hall went Emily and June to Mrs. Warty Thompson's *dum* dum de dum. Ahead of them marched Mama and Daddy, smiling and gay. Emily was too busy trying to stand up in her high heels to join in the laughter of the crowd. There was one good thing, though. Nobody could say she was acting stuck-up.

In front of the judges on the stage, Mama paused and curtsied while Daddy bowed. Emily, anxious to do the right thing, managed a teetery curtsy while June propped her up. Everyone laughed and applauded, which made Emily feel much better, because now she was part of the fun. Her toes ached from being curled up so hard, but that did not matter.

Emily and June circled the hall once more before one of the judges whispered to Mrs. Warty Thompson, who finished the march and then thumped out shave-and-a-haircut-two-bits for good measure, to show that the music really had come to an end.

Uncle Avery held a conference with the judges before he turned to the crowd and shouted, "Hear ye, hear ye, hear ye! The judges have reached a decision!"

"Hooray!" shouted the crowd.

"First prize—" shouted Uncle Avery and waited for the crowd to quiet before he went on. "First prize goes to Mr. and Mrs. Dutch Beesley for being the best-dressed bride and groom in Yamhill County." There was wild applause from the crowd, as Mrs. Beesley, who was wearing an old curtain for a wedding veil and carrying a bouquet of beets and carrots, stepped forward to receive an envelope from the judges.

"And second prize," shouted Uncle Avery, "goes to the younger generation. Emily Bartlett, who has grown out of her dress before growing into her shoes, and her cousin June who offered her such strong support."

There was more wild applause. Emily was astonished. Had she really grown out of her party dress? She must have if Uncle Avery said so—and if she won a prize. At the risk of losing her balance she bent over to look at her hem, and saw that it was much too far above her knees. And her sleeves—now that she thought about them, they were too tight. And the seam that was supposed to be at her waist—it was closer to her ribs. Of course, the dress had felt tight across her chest when she put it on and she could not see much of herself in the mirror at home. . . . Why, she had never looked dressed up at all. She had looked funny, like the rest of the crowd, and Mama knew it all the time.

"We won a prize!" whispered June. "Don't just stand there. Come on!" The two girls somehow reached the stage, where the judges handed them an envelope.

"What is it?" asked Emily, still a little dazed.

June tore open the envelope and pulled out two one-dollar bills. "Look," she said in awe. "Two whole dollars."

"One apiece." Emily could scarcely believe such fortune. A whole dollar! Emily had never before had a whole dollar at one time. Her sitting-still money now added up to over a dollar, but it was all in nickels and not in one piece like this dollar.

"What are you going to do with yours?" asked June.

"Buy Mama a Christmas present," answered Emily.

June looked curiously at her cousin. "How come you said you didn't wear a costume?"

"I was just spoofing," answered Emily airily. "I wanted it to be a surprise."

A man with a violin and another with a cornet joined Mrs. Warty Thompson, and the music for dancing began. Emily tottered over to the chairs along the wall and uncurled her toes. In spite of the excitement she began to feel tired and sleepy, not that she would have mentioned it to anyone. But it was past her bedtime, way past. Other boys and girls were beginning to lie down on the folding chairs, but Emily resolutely watched the dancers and swallowed her yawns until Mama came over and whispered, "Why don't you take a little nap?"

Emily nodded and Mama made her as comfortable as it was possible to make her on three folding chairs. She put Emily's coat under her head for a pillow and spread her own coat over her. This dance was called a fox-trot, which was funny, because Emily was sure foxes did not trot this way. . . .

Emily struggled to keep her eyes open just a little while longer. As she watched the tattered and patched knees of the dancers moving past, it suddenly occurred to her that she now had more than enough money for Mama's eggbeater. She had enough money to buy something else, too.

And Emily knew exactly what she was going to buy. A book for the library! She would ask Mama to send away to Portland for *Black Beauty*, and when it came she would sit right down and read it herself. If it was as good as Muriel said it was, she would read it three times, one right after the other, and then she would give it to the library. Mama would write in the front, "A Gift from Emily Bartlett," and the library would have one more book.

Emily gave up trying to keep her eyes open, and as she drifted off into sleep her last thought was, Maybe times weren't so hard after all, not when a girl like Emily Bartlett could afford to present a book to the library. . . .

9

Emily and Fong Quock

And so the little library grew. Mama sent away for *Black Beauty* and Emily read it three times, even though she did not think it was as good as Muriel said it was. It was a sad book, but that part was all right. Emily enjoyed reading sad things. It was fun to cry over a book, and Mama said wait till she got to *Little Women*. It was the way the horses chatted about their aches and pains that bothered Emily. Horses in Pitchfork neighed, whinnied, or nickered. They did not have long visits with each other about their troubles.

Mama wrote "A Gift from Emily Bartlett" in the front of the book, and the Pitchfork Library had one more volume. It had, in fact, many more books, because Mama had bought them with the money from the hard-times party. The rest of the money would be used to pay Pete Ginty to build some real library shelves. There was even some talk around Pitchfork that the next time there was an election people might vote some money for the library. Right now the trouble was that the library was outgrowing the corner of the Commercial Clubrooms, but never mind. Mama would figure out something. Emily had faith.

One morning in February, Emily was thinking about the library as she sat at the kitchen table with paper, crayons, mucilage, and a bunch of pussy willows she had picked in the pasture. She was making a valentine for her cousin Muriel in Portland.

First Emily folded a piece of paper in half, cut out half a heart, opened the paper, and there was a whole heart. Then with her brown crayon she drew a fence across the middle of the heart. On the fence she squeezed three dots of mucilage and on each dot she pressed a fat pussy-willow blossom. With her black crayon she drew ears and tails on the pussy-willow blossoms. There! She had three furry kittens sitting on a fence. Kittens with fur you could really pet.

The poem came next. This Emily printed in red crayon.

As long as kittens mew
I love you.
Guess who?

It was not as stirring as the poems Miss Plotkin made the class memorize in school—things like, "Listen, my children, and you shall *hear* of the midnight ride of Paul Re*vere*"—but it did rhyme and that was something for a made-up poem. Emily finished the valentine with a red and yellow border.

Mama dried her hands on a huck towel and came to admire Emily's work. "That is a very nice valentine," she said.

Emily was pleased that Mama admired her valentine, but she still had her doubts. "I suppose Muriel is making valentines out of a store-boughten box," she said. She could picture Muriel working at her valentines in the city. She would be using little pieces of pleated paper to attach white paper lace to hearts already printed with roses and bluebirds. When Emily took Muriel's valentine out of the envelope, the lace would jump at her on its little paper springs.

"I suppose so," agreed Mama, "but I think your valentine is much nicer."

This was comforting. Mama knew about a lot of things, because she had gone to school in Chicago before she came out West to be a school teacher. Mama had even been to the opera.

Reassured, Emily stuffed her valentine into an envelope and licked the flap. She would ask Uncle Avery, at the post office, to cancel the stamp by hand instead of cranking the envelope through the cancelling machine, which might squash the pussy-willow kittens.

"You could go to the post office now," said Mama, "and stop at the store for a pound of coffee."

Emily glanced out of the kitchen window. There were a few patches of blue in the gray sky. She would not have to take her umbrella, but she would have to wear her new rubbers, which had been one of her practical Christmas presents.

When Emily reached the corner in front of the farm, she was faced with a choice— to go the long way to the left past the orchard, get her new rubbers muddy, and avoid passing Fong Quock's house, or to go straight ahead the short way on the boardwalk past Fong Quock's house and keep the shiny black newness on her rubbers. Emily loved new things. New boxes of crayons, new Montgomery Ward catalogs, new rubbers.

Emily chose the short way. What if she did see Fong Quock? Since the hard-times party Emily no longer worried about being laughed at. Everyone had laughed at her that night and she had not minded a bit. In spite of her rubbers, which Mama had bought two sizes too large so she would be sure to get the wear out of them, Emily, her valentine clutched in one mittened hand, hippity-hopped along the board sidewalk, making a thumping noise whenever she hit a loose board.

When she came to Fong Quock's house, she saw the old man standing on the front porch studying the weather. He saw her and she saw him, so there was no walking past pretending she was looking up at a bird in a tree or anything like that. Emily's pioneer ancestors would not have been shy about passing Fong Quock's house. Look at all the Indians they had not been afraid to pass as they journeyed across the plains. Emily slowed to a dignified walk, smiled, and bobbed her head.

Fong Quock smiled and bobbed his head back at her.

Well, thought Emily, this is a good system if we don't spend too much time in each other's company. Blithely she went

hippity-hopping on her way.

At the post office she explained about the pussy-willow kittens to Uncle Avery, who was sorting the morning mail. Then she went into Grandpa's store. "Hello, Grandpa," she said, "Mama needs a pound of coffee."

Grandpa was busy writing up a grocery order. "Go ahead and wait on yourself, Emily," he said.

Emily was glad it was coffee she had come for, and not something easy, like a package of powdered sugar or a can of Log Cabin syrup. She hoped the old men who were sitting around the stove chewing tobacco and talking politics while they waited for Uncle Avery to sort the mail would notice her and think, My, the way that girl measures coffee!

Carefully Emily weighed exactly one pound of coffee beans from the bin under the counter—not one bean more or one bean less—and then she dumped them into the red grinder and turned the handle that made the machine chew noisily and spray ground-up coffee into a container, which Emily emptied into a paper bag. Mmm. How good it smelled! So far, none of the old men had paid any attention to her, which was a pity because she had snapped open the paper bag with such a flourish.

But suddenly Emily was paying attention to the old men. One of them was saying, "Did you hear that old Fong Quock is going back to China?"

"Yup," answered another old man, getting up to spit tobacco juice into the stove. "That's what they say."

Emily stared at the old men, waiting for them to say more about this astonishing piece of news. One of the men pulled out his big round watch, opened it, and said, "Looks

like it's about time for the mail to be out."
And then all the old men got up and left the
store.

"Grandpa, is Fong Quock really going
back to China?" Emily asked.

"So I hear," answered Grandpa, adding
up the grocery order.

China! Someone from Pitchfork, Oregon,
was going across the broad Pacific to
China!

"When is he going?" Emily wanted to
know.

"Soon as he can get his affairs straightened out," said Grandpa.

"Is he going to stay there?" Emily asked.

"I expect so," answered Grandpa. "A trip
like that at his age . . ."

"How is he going to get there?" Emily
asked.

"I hear he is going to take the train
to Frisco," said Grandpa. "From there he

will take the boat."

Well! This was exciting! A real world traveler in Pitchfork. Mama always said travel was a wonderful thing. Not that people in Pitchfork did not travel. When Uncle Avery was a soldier during the war, he traveled all the way across the United States to New Jersey, where he peeled potatoes. And one winter before Daddy married Mama, he had a job guarding gold for Wells Fargo. He guarded it on the train all the way down to San Francisco and no bandits ever held up that train, not with Daddy guarding the gold. And almost every day someone took the train to Portland. Emily had been there herself several times and the things she had seen! Streetcars, policemen, a dog wearing a little coat (imagine, a coat on a *dog!*) and best of all, a restaurant where pats of butter were served on tiny doll's plates.

But no one in Pitchfork had ever gone as far as China. Of course a lot of people had come a long way to be in Pitchfork. Mama had come from back East. So had Grandpa and Grandma. And when Grandpa was a little boy *his* mother and father had brought him all the way from England on a sailing vessel. And then there were the pioneer ancestors who had come from Missouri in their covered wagons. But no one ever went back. Once people came to Pitchfork they stayed.

And now Fong Quock was going to China and he wasn't coming back. Emily could hardly wait to tell someone such important news. The first person Emily met outside the post office was Pete Ginty, whose beard looked blacker and bushier than ever.

"Hello there, Emily," said Pete Ginty.

Emily simply had to tell someone the news. "Good morning, Mr. Ginty," she said politely. "Did you know Fong Quock is going all the way back to China?"

Pete Ginty leaned against the wall of the post office, hooked his thumbs in his belt, and looked at Emily. "So I hear," he said. "Fong told me so himself just a few minutes ago. Matter of fact he was carrying a monkey wrench—said he wanted to trade it for a girl about your age to take back to China with him."

Emily did not know how to take this news. She looked at Pete Ginty. His eyes were not smiling. She could not tell about his mouth in all those whiskers. "What for?" she asked suspiciously.

"Because he has only sons and grandsons in China," answered Pete Ginty.

"Oh," was all Emily could say. Did he mean Fong Quock wanted to trade *her* for a monkey wrench to take *her* back to China? My goodness, she didn't want to go to China. Go to China, and leave Mama and Daddy and Grandpa and Grandma? I should say not! Probably Pete Ginty was trying to tease her, but if he was, he gave no sign.

"Yep. Told me so just a few minutes ago," said Pete Ginty. "Well, so long, Emily."

"Good-bye, Mr. Ginty," said Emily faintly as he went into the post office. My goodness! What a terrible thought—to be traded for a monkey wrench. Surely this was all a joke, but Emily could not be sure. She recalled how Pete Ginty used to brag about how he could play the piano, using only the black keys. Daddy said this was just some more of Pete Ginty's humbug, until one day when he came to the sitting-room door to speak to Daddy about cutting some wood in the pasture. He stepped inside to the piano and played *Upidee* all on the black keys. So now Emily did not know what to think, but she was sure about one thing. Mama and Daddy would never trade her for a monkey wrench or even a dozen monkey wrenches.

But now what was she going to do? If she ran into Fong Quock, he might ask her to go back to China with him. Even if he didn't, she might think he did, because he was so hard to understand. And what on earth would she say? If she said, "No thank you, I do not care to go to China," when he had not asked her, he would think her mighty strange.

Clutching her coffee in her mitten-covered hands, Emily walked slowly down Main Street. The next person she came to was old George A. Barbee, whom she saw rather than met, because he was lying on his back under his Ford. My, this was certainly Emily's morning to run into beards! "Good morning, Mr. Barbee," said Emily, bending over to peer at him.

"Morning, Emily," answered the old man, looking out from under his car. There was a dab of grease on his gray beard.

"Did you know Fong Quock is going back to China?" asked Emily, still eager to share the exciting news.

"So I hear." Old George A. tapped at his car with his wrench.

Maybe Emily could find out something from old George A. "I—I heard he wants to trade a monkey wrench for a girl about my age to take back to China," she ventured.

Old George A. stuck his head out from under his car. "Pete Ginty tell you that?" he asked.

"Yes," answered Emily. "Yes, he did." So it was true. Old George A. knew that Pete Ginty knew. Oh dear, now she really would have to avoid Fong Quock.

It was easy to see that the old man was too

busy to talk, so Emily went on. When she came to the corner she paused to make up her mind. The short way, on the boardwalk, to keep the new look on her rubbers? The long way, past the orchard and through the mud, to avoid passing Fong Quock's house? This time Emily chose the long way. She could not expect to keep the new look on her rubbers forever.

Gingerly Emily stepped off the walk onto the muddy road. Oozy mud the color of chocolate sucked at her rubbers. Walking was not easy she soon discovered, because her rubbers were too big. If she lifted her feet too fast, her rubbers stuck in the mud. Emily walked carefully, lifting her toes out of the mud before her heels, so her rubbers would stay on. Mama would think she was never coming with the coffee.

Once Emily forgot and lifted her heel first. Her foot came up and her rubber stayed in the mud. This was a problem. She had to hang on to the coffee, keep her coat up out of the mud, and pull on her sticky rubber while balancing on one foot. It was quite a trick, especially since she was wearing mittens. After that she kept her eyes on the road to find the places that looked the least muddy.

When she came to the blacksmith shop, her friend Mr. Wilcox opened the door and called out, "Hello there, Emily. What do you think you are doing, wading in that mud?"

Emily was embarrassed. "Going home. I've been to the store."

Mr. Wilcox shook his head, as if he could not understand Emily's behavior. This is plain silly, Emily told herself sternly. That Pete Ginty was only trying to tease her. Or was he? She had expected him to tease her the day she Cloroxed the horse, and instead he had helped her. Emily's feet started to fly out from under her, but she managed to grab a bush and at the same time hang on to the coffee. It would never do to drop the coffee in the mud, not with coffee at such a high price these days.

Emily stayed on her feet until she reached the Bartlett property, where she wiped her rubbers on the grass, which was brown and soggy from the long winter rains. She removed her rubbers on the back porch and as she went into the kitchen she called out, "Mama, I'm home."

"All right, Emily," Mama answered from upstairs.

Something caught Emily's eye and made her glance out of the kitchen window. And whom should she see walking along the side of the house but Fong Quock! He was wearing a plaid Mackinaw over his overalls and on his head was a battered old hat. He was carrying a monkey wrench! Emily stared, fascinated, until he turned the corner of the house. When she heard his foot on the back steps she moved fast. Where could she hide? She lifted the lid of the wood box. It was too splintery. The footsteps advanced up the back steps and walked across the porch. Emily darted into the bathroom, closed the door, and leaned against the chill white edge of the second bathtub in Yamhill County.

There was a knock on the back door. Emily held her breath. She heard Mama moving about upstairs. Another knock, harder this time. Mama's heels came tapping down the stairs, down the hall, across the dining room to the back door. "Why hello, Fong Quock," cried Mama. "Won't you come in? I'm sorry to keep you waiting at the door, but I thought Emily was down here." Then Mama called out, "Emily, where are you?"

Emily did not answer. She was leaning against the second bathtub in Yamhill County and that was where she was going to stay. She heard Fong Quock step into the dining room and say something that she could not catch.

"Oh, you're welcome," answered Mama. Outside in the woodshed which was only a few feet from the house Daddy began to chop wood. *Thunk. Thunk. Thunk.*

Between *thunks* Emily could tell that Fong Quock was having a long talk with Mama. She strained her ears, but she could not catch what he was saying. The farm began to seem like an extraordinarily noisy place. The windmill creaked, a cowbell tinkled, a hen told the world how clever it was to lay an egg.

"Why, Fong Quock!" exclaimed Mama. "Are you sure—"

Thunk. Thunk.

Emily opened the bathroom door and listened, waiting to hear Mama say, "Why, no, I wouldn't dream of letting Emily go all the way to China." *Thunk. Thunk.* She thought the old man said something about "many fliends" and "all likee me," but she was not sure. She did wish he would speak up.

"What a wonderful thing for you to do!" exclaimed Mama unexpectedly.

What was wonderful, Emily wondered, straining to catch Mama's next words.

"—and what it will mean to Emily!" she heard Mama say. "It will open a whole new world to her."

Emily was shocked. A whole new world? Could that new world be—China? Was Mama *accepting* Fong Quock's offer to take her to China? Mama had always said travel was a wonderful thing . . . but to send her only daughter and Grandpa's only granddaughter all the way to China. . . . But Emily was sure she had heard her mother correctly. Mama had said, "It will open a whole new world to her."

And now Mama was saying, "I can't wait to tell Emily. She will be so excited she won't know what to do."

Oh, I will, will I, thought Emily indignantly. No, I won't, because I *do not want to go to China*. Mama didn't need to sound so happy.

Thunk. Thunk.

"Where did that girl go?" said Mama. "She was here just a minute ago. Emily!"

Emily did not budge.

"I guess she has gone out to the barn," said Mama.

Emily could hear her mother and Fong Quock walking toward the back door. The door was opened.

"We shall miss you, Fong Quock. Everyone will," said Mama, "but we will never forget what you have done."

"Goo'-bye, goo'-bye," called Fong Quock,

as he went down the steps.

Mama closed the door and returned to the kitchen.

Emily was not scared anymore. She was mad. Just plain mad. Mama wasn't going to send her off to China, because she wasn't going to go. That was all there was to it. She was *not* going to go. Emily burst out of the bathroom. "I don't care what you say, Mama, I won't go!"

Mama looked startled to see Emily appear so suddenly from the bathroom. "Go where?" she asked.

Emily's eye fell on the monkey wrench lying on the kitchen table among her crayons and pussy willows. "To China with Fong Quock," said Emily. "I don't care if you did trade me for a monkey wrench and I don't care if you do think everybody should travel!"

Mama sat down weakly on a kitchen chair. She looked both baffled and amused.

"Emily," she said, "will you please stop acting as mad as a wet hen and tell me what under the sun it is you are talking about."

"About sending me to China," said Emily. What else could she be talking about? "Pete Ginty told me Fong Quock wanted to trade a monkey wrench for a girl about my age to take back to China, because he had only sons and grandsons there."

Mama stared at Emily with a look that was a mixture of love, exasperation, and amusement. "Oh, Emily, the way you let your imagination run away with you!" she exclaimed.

Emily calmed down and glanced once more at the monkey wrench. "But Pete Ginty said—"

"Oh, that man!" snapped Mama. "You should know better than to believe any of his yarns."

"But he really can play the piano on the

black keys . . ." answered Emily uncertainly.

"Emily, Fong Quock came here to return the monkey wrench your father loaned him. Pete Ginty was just teasing you," said Mama. "You should have known that."

Emily felt better, but she did not see how she was supposed to know Pete Ginty had been teasing her. It was so hard to tell about grown-ups sometimes. "But you said it would open a whole new world to me," she said doubtfully.

"I was talking about the world of books. Many books instead of a few from the state library." Mama smiled at Emily. "I didn't tell you the other reason why Fong Quock came here."

"What other reason?" asked Emily. Whatever it was, it must be good news, because Mama looked so excited and happy.

"He said that times are so hard that he

can't find anyone to buy his house, so he has decided to give it to the people of Pitchfork to use for a library!" Mama smiled at Emily. "Now what do you think of that?"

"Mama!" cried Emily. "A whole house?"

"A whole house," answered Mama, "and the best part is that since we have a house for the library now, I know the people of Pitchfork will vote money for the library in the next election."

Emily couldn't think of a thing to say. A real library in a house all by itself! Fong Quock's little house, the closest to her own. How handy!

"Poor old fellow," Mama remarked sadly. "He says he has many friends here and that everyone likes him, but just the same I know he must have been lonely many times."

"Why, Mama?" asked Emily. He did not look lonely to her. He always went to church, and she often saw him on Main Street talking to people.

"Because when he came to Oregon to seek his fortune as a young man, he settled in a strange town and had to learn a new language and new customs. He must have been homesick many times, even though in the early days there were other Chinese who came here to seek their fortune."

Emily felt ashamed of herself for avoiding such a nice old man, a remarkable man who was giving a whole house for the library. And to think he had been lonely right here in Pitchfork. Emily looked at her crayons and mucilage and pussy willows still scattered on the kitchen table. "Mama, do you think Fong Quock would like a valentine?" she asked.

Mama smiled. "I am sure he would."

That settled it. Emily went right to work with paper and crayons. She squeezed three drops of mucilage on her crayon fence and pressed three pussy willows on the dots. Then with red crayon she printed:

As long as kittens mew,
Fong Quock, I love you.
Guess who?

In tiny letters down in one corner she printed her initials before she slipped the valentine into an envelope.

Then Emily put on her coat and her rubbers again and went hippity-hopping down the boardwalk all the way to Fong Quock's house. She tiptoed up to his porch, soon to be the porch of the library, where she intended to slip her valentine under the door. Now she discovered the pussy-willow kittens were too fat, so she leaned her valentine against the door where the old man could not miss it when he came out.

As Emily was tiptoeing down the walk, Fong Quock, who must have been watching her all the time, opened the door and picked up the valentine. He opened the envelope and studied the kittens with a smile on his wrinkled old face. Then he looked at Emily and smiled and nodded his head. Emily smiled and nodded her head. Fong Quock waved and Emily waved back.

With a light heart Emily went hippity-hopping on her way home. This remarkable man, who had given his house for a library and who was going to travel all the way to China, knew that someone in Pitchfork was thinking of him.

And just think—now Pitchfork was going to have a real library and she, Emily Bartlett, was the girl who almost a year ago had licked the stamp that went on the envelope that held the letter to the state library that started the whole thing.

Yes, Emily decided, she was pretty lucky to have the kind of imagination that ran away.

BEVERLY CLEARY is one of America's most popular authors. Born in McMinnville, Oregon, she lived on a farm in Yamhill until she was six and then moved to Portland. After college, as the children's librarian in Yakima, Washington, she was challenged to find stories for non-readers. She wrote her first book, HENRY HUGGINS, in response to a boy's question, "Where are the books about kids like us?"

Mrs. Cleary's books have earned her many prestigious awards, including the American Library Association's Laura Ingalls Wilder Award, presented in recognition of her lasting contribution to children's literature. Her DEAR MR. HENSHAW was awarded the 1984 John Newbery Medal, and both RAMONA QUIMBY, AGE 8 and RAMONA AND HER FATHER have been named Newbery Honor Books. In addition, her books have won more than thirty-five statewide awards based on the votes of her young readers. Her characters, including Henry Huggins, Ellen Tebbits, Otis Spofford, and Beezus and Ramona Quimby, as well as Ribsy, Socks, and Ralph S. Mouse, have delighted children for generations. Mrs. Cleary lives in coastal California.

Visit Beverly Cleary on the World Wide Web at www.beverlycleary.com.

1

Mitchell's Skateboard

Mitchell Huff's day began like any other summer day—with a squabble with his twin sister Amy. At breakfast Amy grabbed a cereal box top and said, "I'm going to send away for the plastic harmonica that looks like an ear of corn."

"Oh, no you don't!" said Mitchell. "It's my turn to get the box top."

"It is not!" said Amy. "You got the last one."

"But it wasn't a good box top," said Mitchell. "How come you get all the good box tops?"

"I don't," said Amy. "You sent away for the pedometer."

"Yes, but it broke the first time I used it," said Mitchell.

"That wasn't my fault," said Amy.

"It's no fair," said Mitchell. "You always grab the good box tops, and then don't send away for things."

"Be quiet, both of you," said Mrs. Huff,

"or I shall serve hot oatmeal every morning, three hundred sixty-five days of the year, and you won't have any box tops to send away."

Mr. Huff, who had to catch a bus to the city, glanced at his watch and said, "That ought to settle this morning's squabble."

"Okay, Mom. You win," Mitchell said amiably.

"Oatmeal, ick," said Amy.

After breakfast Mitchell went out to the patio to work on the skateboard he was building out of an old board and a roller skate while Amy went to her room and began to play her cello. That's funny, thought Mitchell, sawing the board in two, nobody told her to practice. There was something familiar about the catchy tune his sister was playing, and Mitchell grinned when he recognized that it was not her lesson, but the music from a television commercial. That Amy!

In a few minutes the cello was silent, but Amy's tune ran through Mitchell's head half the morning. He was pounding the last nail around the half of the skate fastened to the front of the board when Amy came out the back door.

"I thought I heard Marla come through the gate," Amy said. She picked a dandelion that had gone to seed in a flower bed and held it up to examine it more closely.

Mitchell gave the nail a final bang with the hammer and sat back on his heels, waiting for Amy to say something about his skateboard, but Amy was looking at the ball of dandelion fluff as if she found it a thing of magic and, while Mitchell watched, she closed her eyes to make a wish.

Mitchell looked at his sister standing there in her playclothes with her knees bruised, her brown hair falling to her shoulders, and her summer freckles bright in the September sunshine. Her lips were puckered beside the dandelion's white head as if they had been drawn up by a string. He saw her chest rise

4

as she drew a deep breath and held it for a moment.

Suddenly the temptation was too great for Mitchell. Gathering his breath he rose and moved swiftly and silently across the concrete on his rubber soles.

Whoof! Mitchell blew as hard as he could and sent every one of Amy's dandelion seeds dancing off into the sunshine.

Amy's eyes flew open, and for a moment she stared at the empty stem in her hand. Then with a yell of rage she flung it onto the patio. "Mitchell Huff!" she shrieked. "You spoiled my wish! I'll get you for this!"

Have fun reading great books
by beloved author
★ BeVeRLy CLeaRy ★

HarperTrophy®
An Imprint of HarperCollinsPublishers

www.harpercollinschildrens.com